MAIN COURSE

Fargo saw Carol disappear under the surface, and dove past the alligator's open jaws into the water. The gator turned instantly with one whip of his huge tail, but Fargo was moving at him from the side. The huge amphibian's jaws snapped open and shut as he cast around for his prey. Fargo flung himself onto the gator's back. He clung with all his strength as the beast rolled in the water, using his tail to turn over and over, trying to dislodge the object on top of him.

Fargo drew a last, deep breath and held it as the gator dived a few feet and shot to the surface. But as the huge amphibian started to spin again, Fargo felt his muscles weakening. He knew he'd never be able to hold on for another fury of spinning . . . and where was Carol?

BLAZING NEW TRAILS
WITH SKYE FARGO

☐ **THE TRAILSMAN #107: GUNSMOKE GULCH by Jon Sharpe.** Skye Fargo blasts a white-slaving ring apart and discovers that a beauty named Annie has a clue to a gold mine worth slaying for—a proposition that makes Skye ready to blaze a trail through a gunsmoke screen of lethal lies.   (168038—$3.50)

☐ **THE TRAILSMAN #109: LONE STAR LIGHTNING by Jon Sharpe.** Skye Fargo on a Texas manhunt with two deadly weapons—a blazing gun and a fiery female.   (168801—$3.50)

☐ **THE TRAILSMAN #110: COUNTERFEIT CARGO by Jon Sharpe.** The pay was too good for Skye Fargo to turn down, so he's guiding a wagon train loaded with evil and heading for hell.   (168941—$3.50)

☐ **THE TRAILSMAN #111: BLOOD CANYON by Jon Sharpe.** Kills Fast, the savage Cheyenne medicine man, hated Skye Fargo like poison. And when Skye followed a perverse pair of paleskin fugitives into redskin hands, Kills Fast wasn't about to live up to his name.   (169204—$3.50)

☐ **THE TRAILSMAN #112: THE DOOMSDAY WAGONS by Jon Sharpe.** Skye Fargo follows a trail of corpses on a trip through hell for a showdown with marauding redskins.   (169425—$3.50)

☐ **THE TRAILSMAN #113: SOUTHERN BELLES by Jon Sharpe.** The Trailsman had plenty of bullets in his gunbelt when a Mississippi paddle-wheeler found itself in a mist of mystery as ripe young beauties were plucked from its cabins.   (169635—$3.50)

THE
TRAILSMAN
114

THE
TAMARIND
TRAIL

by

Jon Sharpe

A SIGNET BOOK

SIGNET
Published by the Penguin Group
Penguin Books USA Inc., 375 Hudson Street,
New York, New York 10014, U.S.A.
Penguin Books Ltd, 27 Wrights Lane,
London W8 5TZ, England
Penguin Books Australia Ltd, Ringwood,
Victoria, Australia
Penguin Books Canada Ltd, 2801 John Street,
Markham, Ontario, Canada L3R 1B4
Penguin Books (N.Z.) Ltd, 182–190 Wairau Road,
Auckland 10, New Zealand

Penguin Books Ltd, Registered Offices:
Harmondsworth, Middlesex, England

First published by Signet, an imprint of New American Library,
a division of Penguin Books USA Inc.

First Printing, June, 1991
10 9 8 7 6 5 4 3 2 1

The first chapter of this book originally appeared in *Southern Belles*, the one hundred-thirteenth volume in this series.

 REGISTERED TRADEMARK—MARCA REGISTRADA

Printed in the United States of America

PUBLISHER'S NOTE
This is a work of fiction. Names, characters, places, and incidents either are the product of the author's imagination or are used fictitiously, and any resemblance to actual persons, living or dead, events, or locales is entirely coincidental.

The Trailsman

Beginnings . . . they bend the tree and they mark the man. Skye Fargo was born when he was eighteen. Terror was his midwife, vengeance his first cry. Killing spawned Skye Fargo, ruthless, cold-blooded murder. Out of the acrid smoke of gunpowder still hanging in the air, he rose, cried out a promise never forgotten.

The Trailsman they began to call him all across the West: searcher, scout, hunter, the man who could see where others only looked, his skills for hire but not his soul, the man who lived each day to the fullest, yet trailed each tomorrow. Skye Fargo, the Trailsman, the seeker who could take the wildness of a land and the wanting of a woman and make them his own.

*Florida, 1860, just east
of the Ocala forest, where lush
beauty was a trap and death
waited for the unwary . . .*

1

The big man with the lake-blue eyes swore silently as he peered across the saloon without putting down the piece of roast chicken he was enjoying. Trouble, he knew, could come at unexpected times and in all kinds of shapes and ways. This time, trouble came with short brown hair, and a smudged face which was nonetheless perkily pretty. The small, wiry figure had high, round breasts which even the loose tan shirt couldn't conceal, jeans and boots and a holster at her hip. He had seen her as she entered the saloon, a pugnacious scruffiness to her. She walked to where six men were playing poker at one of the large round tables.

He had started to return to his meal when her voice cut through the low murmur of the saloon.

"Goddamn you, Max Garson, what'd you do with Una?" she barked. The big man saw her plant her feet as though she were a gunfighter. The saloon instantly fell silent and the bartender began to back away from the front of the bar. The six poker players had turned in their chairs to look at her, all except the one who faced her directly. A big man, at least two hundred pounds, with a heavy-featured face, thick lips, a wide, flattened nose, beetling black eyebrows and unruly black hair, he spoke in a deep, growling voice.

"Who are you, girlie?"

"Annie Dowd. I'm Una's cousin and I want to know what you did with her," the girl said.

"I don't know anything about your damn cousin."

"Liar, stinking rotten liar," the girl shot back. "I know what you are, Garson. You're a kidnapping, woman-stealing, stinking, rotten slave-trading bastard."

Skye Fargo put down his piece of chicken after one more bite as the man's eyes grew narrow.

"You've a real nasty little mouth, girlie," Max Garson said as he pushed to his feet.

"Draw on me, Garson. Come on, I dare you," the scruffy little figure threw at him. "I can put an end to you right here and now. Go on, draw."

Fargo frowned. She was plainly furious, and anger was making her either damn confident or damn dumb. It was probably the latter, he decided. But Garson didn't draw, he noticed. The man had been challenged and he'd every right, but he didn't move his gun arm. Instead, an oily smile turned his thick lips. "You must be kidding," he said.

"Try me, damn you, Garson. Try me," Annie Dowd flung back. "You're a damn coward, too."

Fargo saw the man's heavy-featured face harden. "You need some manners, girlie," he growled, and Fargo's peripheral vision caught the figure move away from the bar. The man moved silently in a half-circle to come up behind the girl, a lean, lanky figure with a mean mouth and small black eyes, clothed in black Levi's and a black shirt. Annie Dowd's attention was concentrated on Garson and she neither saw nor felt the man come up behind her until her arms were pinned to her sides from behind. She tried to twist away but the long, lanky figure had her pinned tightly, his arms wrapped entirely around her.

"Goddamn, let go of me, you bastard," Annie Dowd spit out as she tried to free herself and failed again as the black-clothed figure pulled her up straight.

"Get her gun," Max Garson ordered, and one of

the other poker players stepped forward and lifted the six-gun from the girl's holster, a .44 Allen & Wheelock army six-shot single-action piece. Garson's oily smile touched his thick lips again as his eyes bored into Annie Dowd. "Now we'll be taking you into the back and see how big your mouth really is," he said while the others around him sniggered.

Fargo let a deep sigh escape him as he rose and in two long strides crossed to behind the lanky figure holding the girl, the end of the big Colt pressed against the back of the man's neck. "Let her go and nobody gets hurt," he said, and felt the man stiffen. The man hesitated and Fargo let him hear the click of the Colt's hammer being drawn back. The man released his grip on Annie Dowd and she tore away instantly as Fargo stepped back and holstered the Colt.

The man turned to stare at him, ice in his small eyes. "Who the hell are you, mister?" Fargo heard Max Garson growl.

"Nobody," Fargo said.

"Then you ought to mind your own business."

"I'd like to do that. I'd like to finish my meal," Fargo said pleasantly. "So give the little lady her gun back and let her go her way."

"You just finished your meal, buster. Get the hell out of here or Jack's goin' to carve you into little pieces," Garson said.

Fargo glanced at the long, lanky man and saw him draw a long-bladed dagger from inside his shirt. Fargo's eyes flicked to the table and saw that Garson and two of the others had their guns drawn and leveled at him.

Annie Dowd, concern in her eyes, had backed a few paces away. "I'll go. I don't want anybody hurt on my account," she said.

"You're not going anywhere, you little bitch," Garson snapped. "And your friend's goin' to learn about butting in to other people's business."

"He's not my friend. I never saw him before. Leave him out of this," Annie Dowd said.

Fargo smiled inwardly. She had a sense of justice. She was trying to take him off the hook. But Garson wasn't about to let it turn that way. He felt he had the upper hand and he'd use it. But he'd not expect boldness, none of them would. He smiled as he spoke.

"You stupid son of a bitch with the knife, I'm waiting for you," Fargo said, and the long, lanky man's small eyes widened. He threw a glance at Garson.

"Cut his damn head off, Jack," Garson said, and the lanky figure moved quickly, on the balls of his feet as he came toward the big man. Fargo backed, circled, his eyes on the man's hands. The lean body would be quick, he knew, but he'd favor fast slashing motions. That was in his body movements and the way he held the long-handled dagger. His first lunging slash was a slicing blow delivered sidearm. Fargo leaned backward and let the knifeblade almost swipe his stomach. He countered with a left hook he knew would appear feeble and then circled again.

The man whirled, slashed again, and once more Fargo let the blow almost land. Garson and the other two men still had their guns leveled at him. If he tried to draw, they'd open fire, so he kept his hand away from the holster as the lean figure came in with another blow, a straight-armed slash this time that grazed Fargo's shoulder. Fargo dropped into a crouch, weaved, and with a grin, his opponent lashed out in a long arc with the blade. Fargo ducked one slash, ducked another, and retreated. The man rushed after him, overconfident now, lunging and slashing. Fargo continued to stay in a half-crouch as he ducked to the right and the left.

Fargo knew he'd not be able to avoid many more

of the lunging slashes, the half-crouch allowing him only to twist and duck. It was exactly what he wanted the knife-wielder to think. And he was right. He could only avoid a few more lunges. But he stayed in the crouch, ducking away from a slice of the dagger that tore his shirt open at the shoulder. He sensed the table at his back and the chair alongside it. He twisted away toward it, backed, and came against the chair. He flung his arms out as he appeared to stumble off-balance, a moment of fright on his face. The man gave a cry of triumph as he leapt in, but Fargo's hand had closed around the leg of the chair as he went backward. He swung it in a short arc and his opponent's legs crashed into it. The man fell forward, his momentum and balance disrupted. It was the split second Fargo waited for, and he brought his fist down in a thunderous pile-driver blow that landed on the man's wrist.

The knife dropped from his hand as he untangled himself from the chair. Fargo dropped low and scooped the long-bladed dagger up in one hand as the man charged to get his hand on it. Fargo turned the knife upward, and the long, lanky figure tried to halt his momentum but he couldn't do it. Fargo saw his mouth fall open as he impaled himself on the blade. He started to fall forward and the long blade slid into his abdomen to the hilt. Fargo pushed himself up, wrapped one arm around the man, and spun him around to face the others. Fargo's Colt was in his hand as he held the man in front of him, a sagging, lifeless shield.

"Throw your guns down, gents," Fargo said, still holding the lifeless form with one hand. Garson dropped his gun and the other two men followed his example. Fargo flung the long, lean form away from him as his eyes bored into Garson. "He's yours," Fargo said.

"Take Jack outside," Garson said.

Two of the poker players stepped forward, lifted the lifeless form, and carried it from the saloon.

Fargo's eyes had turned the frigid blue of an ice floe as he stared at Garson. "Give the girl her gun back," he said.

"Certainly." Garson nodded, and one of the men stepped forward to hand the long-barreled Allen & Wheelock back to Annie. "Seems everyone got a mite too excited," Garson said soothingly.

"Maybe," Fargo said, and his eyes stayed on the heavy-featured man as he spoke to the small, wiry form beside him. "You get on out of here now," he said.

"I want to explain to you, mister," she said.

"I want to finish eating," Fargo said, his voice hardening. "Get out of here."

She hesitated, and a quick glance showed him her smudged face carried concern and uncertainty. But she turned on her heel and strode from the saloon.

Fargo backed to his table, sat down, and placed the Colt beside the plate. "Now I'll be finishing my meal," he said to Garson. "I don't like to be disturbed when I'm eating, especially twice. It makes me very irritable." He leaned back and picked up his piece of chicken and saw Garson motion to his men as he sat down around the poker table again.

Fargo had only three bites of his chicken left and he finished them, downed the last of the bourbon in the shot glass, and sat for a moment with his hand on the Colt, thoughts dancing through his head. It was his first visit to the saloon, his first visit to the town. Snakebird, they called it. Indeed, it was his first visit to the state and he'd already seen that it was a place far different than any he'd even been.

Yet some things never changed, he grunted. Bullies and killers were the same all over. Scenery had little effect on the behavior of men. Or of women. Good was a constant beyond time and place, and evil was evil no matter what the backdrop. Fargo's eyes went to Garson and the others at the table. They had renewed their card game, but the scruffy little girl had flung scathing accusations. Max Garson wasn't the kind to ignore them. Resumption of the poker game was a deception and Fargo decided to prepare his move first. He rose, paid for the meal, and casually walked past the cardplayers. He felt Garson's eyes following him as he left the saloon.

Outside, the night was warm, the air faintly smelling of flowers and honeysuckle. Each night carried the same sweet smell, he had found. The magnificent Ovaro waited at the hitching post, its jet-black fore-and-hind-quarters a stark contrast to the pure white of its midsection. He swung onto the horse and rode past two low-roofed buildings. He spied the small alleyway between the next two and backed the horse into the narrow space. The street curved and he could see the saloon. He hadn't more than five minutes to wait when he saw the three men hurry from the saloon, climb onto their horses, and go down the street at a fast canter. Garson wasn't one of them, but the three were among his poker-playing cronies.

Fargo moved the Ovaro from the narrow alleyway and, staying back far enough not to be picked up, followed the three riders. As soon as the men left town, they rode along a narrow road that bordered a thick forest of sweetgum, palmetto palm, tupelo, and many other kinds of trees whose names Fargo had yet to discover. Hanging forests, he'd already come to call them, filled with lush flowers and tendrils and vines and always that slightly heavy, sweet smell of tropical blossoms. The horsemen were not following tracks, he noted. They were moving much too fast for that. They knew where the girl was headed and were riding to catch up to her.

Fargo's lips pulled back in a grimace. He wouldn't get involved in anything more than saving her hide. She had a kind of recklessness that came only from honesty and she probably deserved a helping hand. But she'd have to fight the rest of her battles herself. He'd come here on a job—no final agreement yet, but they'd sent a handsome piece of traveling money. He'd not let himself be sidetracked by anything else, not here in this state they called Florida, a place entirely new to him. He'd told them that in the letter he'd sent back, but they wanted to meet with him anyway. So he had come after finishing breaking trail for a new haulage route into Tennessee.

The road ended as it veered from the forest and became a level expanse of open land, and his thoughts broke off. The moonlight let him see the girl riding some hundred yards ahead. He saw the three pursuers pick up speed. She turned in the saddle as she heard the sound of their horses and put her mount into a full gallop in an effort to outrun her pursuers. But her horse was a small mount with short strides and the three men were quickly catching up to her. Fargo saw a cluster of low hawthorns take shape to the right, and the girl headed for them. Two shots rang out and she began to veer her horse in one direction, then another as she continued to ride for the hawthorn.

But she was losing ground with each maneuver. The three men were closing ground quickly now. Fargo saw her skid her horse to a halt and bring the horse down to the ground. She flattened herself low behind the horse's thick-chested body and fired off a shot at the nearest rider. It was a trick that worked best against a horde of onrushing pursuers who were going to charge by. But these three separated to circle her and came at her from three different directions. Fargo reined to a halt, pulled the big Sharps from its saddle case, and lifted the rifle to his shoulder.

He chose the rider who'd circled behind her, drew a bead on the man, followed him for an instant as he charged closer, and fired. The figure toppled from his horse with his arms flung out. The other two reined to a halt in surprise and peered across the open land.

Annie Dowd fired and Fargo saw the one to his left fly from his horse. The third one wheeled his horse and raced away. Annie fired another two shots after him, but both missed as he disappeared into the night.

Fargo walked the Ovaro forward as the girl rose and let her horse regain its feet. She had just finished reloading her revolver when he reached her, and she looked up at him with surprise and gratefulness showing through her smudged face. "That's one more I owe you," she said.

"I'd say you made Garson real mad at you," Fargo said. "You did call him some rough things."

"He wants to stop me from meeting with someone due in town tomorrow," Annie Dowd said. "I don't think he'll try again tonight."

"I'd guess not," Fargo said as he swung to the ground. She was a small, wiry figure. The high round breasts under the tan shirt were the only womanly thing about her. For the rest, she gave the appearance of a pugnacious waif.

"Now I can do that explaining to you," she said.

"No," Fargo said abruptly, and she frowned and looked almost hurt.

"My place is a half-mile on. I thought I could explain while we rode," she said, and still looked hurt. "I owe you that much."

"I'm sorry, it's just that I'm here on a job and I'm not about to get involved in anything else. There's no point in my knowing more."

She half-shrugged, the disappointment still in her

face. "Whatever you want," she murmured. "You've a name, though."

"No reason to go into that, either. Let's just leave it as it is. I'm glad I was able to help tonight," Fargo said.

She met his eyes with her own, direct stare. "I am real grateful to you, for back at the saloon and for just now," Annie Dowd said.

"Good enough. I don't expect you'll have any more trouble tonight, but I'll stay the night with you if you want," he offered.

"I'm not that grateful," she snapped, flaring at once.

"Didn't mean that." He smiled. "You're a thorny little package, aren't you?"

"I know men," she said, drawing an air of loftiness around her that didn't fit right.

He studied her with a long glance. "I don't think you know a damn thing about men," he said evenly.

She bristled again. "I know that if you're nice to them, they'll come running with only one thing on their minds," she said, and he laughed. "Well, it's true," she snapped.

"Often enough," he conceded. "Well, you be careful about being nice and being too sure of yourself."

"Meaning what exactly?" she frowned.

"Meaning it may not be healthy to go around challenging people to draw on you."

"You mean Garson? I'd have won," she said. No false bravado, no bragging in her voice, he decided, and he smiled. Overconfidence could be as fatal as bravado.

"Good luck to you, Annie Dowd," he said as he pulled himself onto the Ovaro.

"Thanks again," she said. "I still owe you that explanation. Maybe next time we meet."

"I don't expect there'll be a next time," Fargo said.

"I do," she said flatly. "I'm sure of it."

"Why?"

"I just know. I've a way of feeling things like that," she said.

He waved as he rode away and saw her swing onto her horse. He slowed when he reached the road that led back to town. The young woman's words stayed with him as he rode. He hoped this was one of the times she'd be wrong. She was trouble the first moment he'd seen her, and she was still trouble. The worst kind. The kind that didn't mean any harm. The kind that just dropped problems into your lap without asking anything. The kind that left it up to you to say no to yourself. The worst kind.

2

He slept the night in a small arbor off the road back to town and woke to the humid, damp heat of morning. Little streams ran through the land like veins, and he leisurely washed and dried himself in the sun that filtered down through the trailing vines of the trees. Dressed, he found a pineapple, cut it apart, and breakfasted on its sweetness while he watched a spectacular parade of colors on the birds that flitted and perched nearby. He saw tiny hummingbirds of striking brilliance, parrots in shimmering green, red, and blue, giant macaws in their pure white and brilliant headpieces, purple gallinules and the painted bunting, a Jacob's coat with wings.

But the flowers made even the gaudy plumage of the birds seem drab, an array of every color and hue imaginable. It was easy to see why the Spaniards under Ponce de León had named it Florida, land of the flowers. But with the lush beauty there was sudden death, often also cloaked in beauty such as the pitcher plant and the coral snake. Then there were the cottonmouths and diamondbacks, the great and undiscriminating alligators, and the deadly scorpions. Even the innocent-appearing sawgrass could kill, its rough stems covered with barbs that could cut and slice like the sharpest knife. The Seminoles has used the beds of sawgrass to stand off both the U.S. Army and Navy, a plant only an alligator could touch without suffering terrible cuts.

The combined military forces had never completely defeated the Seminoles. The tribe had split up into small groups that went their own ways, remained hidden, undefeated, and mostly undetected. By their actions and presence they were a denial of any victory the government proclaimed. The climbing sun broke into his musings and he climbed into the saddle and began to make his way toward the town. The meeting had been fixed at the Snakebird Inn. He rode into town under the late-morning sun. He cast a glance around when he reached town for Max Garson, but he didn't see the man or any of his cronies. He passed the saloon, quiet in the late-morning sun.

The Snakebird Inn tried for an air of faded elegance, with tall lanterns beside the entrance and a spacious drawing room. A long overhang had been built over the hitching post to keep the horses out of the direct rays of the sun. But faded wallpaper and cracked and peeling paint destroyed the bow toward elegance. A young man in a green vest greeted him as he entered. "Name's Fargo," the Trailsman said. "I'm meeting some folks from the Raynall Company. They show up yet?"

"They're waiting in the drawing room," the youth said, and Fargo entered the large room with two couches and half a dozen stuffed chairs scattered about. Two men rose to greet him. Just behind them stood a young woman.

"Skye Fargo?" one of the men said, a middle-aged man with graying hair and wearing a traveling suit.

"Bull's-eye," Fargo said as he accepted the man's outstretched hand.

"I'm George Evans, vice president of Raynall and Company," the man said. He turned to the young woman who stepped forward. "This is Carol Siebert, our chief executive, and Tom Riggs, general manager."

Fargo nodded at Riggs, a man younger by some ten years than Evans, and returned his eyes to the young woman. In her middle twenties, he guessed, she wore a tailored shirt with long sleeves that pulled tight around full breasts. He took in dusty-blond hair, a face that was patrician in its good looks, an aquiline nose, slightly flared at the nostrils, muted blue eyes that were somehow nonetheless sharp, and finely molded lips. A straight black skirt couldn't hide a tall and willowy figure with a narrow waist and long-lined thighs. Carol Siebert offered a smile that was absolutely correctly polite, but her muted blue eyes lingered on the chiseled handsomeness of the big man's face.

"I hope you're not too surprised at finding a woman as part of our delegation," she said.

"Not much surprises me," Fargo said. "And I've never minded being around a good-looking woman."

Her smile took on a shade more warmth. "So I heard," she said, and he felt his brows lift. "In our search for you we heard many things," she explained.

"Things get exaggerated," Fargo said.

"Modesty?" Carol Siebert asked with a touch of cool amusement.

"Politeness," he said, and she smiled again. George Evans motioned to one of the chairs and Fargo folded his big frame into it as Carol Siebert sat down opposite him. She kept her knees turned slightly to one side and held tightly together. Proper manners with a touch of primness, he decided.

"We contacted you because we heard you were the very best, and that's what we need," Evans began. "Even though you told us this was new territory to you."

"I wanted you to know that in new country things

sometimes take longer. Breaking trail is always new country in a way, but it helps if you know the surrounding territory," Fargo said.

"I'm sure you're our man, not that I understand what makes a great trailsman," Evans said.

"Two things," Fargo said, and added nothing further.

"Would you like to tell us what they are?" Carol Siebert said, amusement shining in her blue eyes again.

"Same things that make a good lover. Knowing how to read the signs you see and the ones you don't see," he answered, and smiled inwardly at the two tiny dots of color that came into her patrician cheeks. "Just what kind of trail am I supposed to find for you?" he said, including the three of them in the question.

"We want you to find the president of our company, James Raynall," Evans said. "He came here convinced there were rich mineral deposits in this region. He wanted to explore deep into the forests and back country. He carried a thousand dollars with him and we've not heard from him since he left."

"How long ago was that?" Fargo queried.

"Going onto two years now," the man said, and Fargo allowed a moment of surprise to cross his face.

"And you're just getting concerned now?" he asked.

"We've been concerned a long time. We understood his initial silence. These things take time and communication facilities hardly exist around here," Evans said. "But we grew more concerned as time wore on. Now it's reached a point where we can't operate the company and make the decisions that have to be made without a president."

"We have to know whether he's still alive or not. We can't run the company unless we know," Carol Siebert broke in.

"A man comes out here all by himself to explore

for precious minerals? Sounds pretty damn strange," Fargo remarked.

"You had to know James Raynall," Evans answered. "He could find what he wanted to find without a lot of digging equipment."

Carol Siebert broke in again. "I was James Raynall's personal assistant. He's a brilliant metallurgist, a brilliant executive, a man of vision and imagination. He is also a very moody man, an introspective man, given to fits of depression. We were worried when he went away on this exploration, but he insisted on going alone. He said he wanted to get away by himself and combine vacation and business."

"Tell me something more about the James Raynall company," Fargo said.

"We're development investors, mining, chemicals, land, haulage, almost anything. We invest in the things we develop and in things others bring to us," Evans said. "We're based right where Georgia, Alabama, and Florida meet at the southeast juncture."

"It was James Raynall's idea to go down here exploring. He was the only one with any knowledge of this country. He lived near here as a boy, he told us," Riggs put in.

"Sounds as though you're looking to find a needle in a haystack," Fargo remarked.

"Not completely. He gave us a general idea of where he was going to go," Riggs said. "It started here and went south into the Ocala Forest."

"That'll help some but not a hell of a lot," Fargo said.

"You have our offer. Say yes and you can start right away," Evans said.

Fargo sat back, his lips pursed as he thought. The offer they'd written to him had not been the kind a man turns down. He was turning his answer in his head when a figure strode into the room and a voice cut into his thoughts. "I'm looking for the Trailsman . . . Skye Fargo," it said, and he looked up to see the small, compact figure. Her short brown hair was still uncombed, though her face was no longer smudged, her tan shirt, jeans, and boots were the same, her manner still as pugnacious. She halted in surprise when she saw him.

"You're interrupting a private meeting, young woman," Evans said, rising to his feet.

Annie Dowd took her eyes from the big man in the chair. "I told you, I'm looking for Skye Fargo," she said.

"You found him," Fargo said, and saw her eyes grow wider as she turned to him.

"I've got a job for you," she said.

"Now, just a moment," Evans said, his voice rising. "I told you, you're interrupting a private meeting and he already has a job."

"Whoa, there," Fargo said as he rose. "I haven't agreed to anything yet."

"Well, you've as good as agreed. You came to meet with us," Evans protested.

"You sent me traveling money to come listen," Fargo said.

"I'll better anything they offered," Annie Dowd cut in.

Evans started toward her, his face flushed. "Get out. This is our meeting. You've no business here," he said.

Annie Dowd's right hand dropped toward her holster, her feet planted firmly. "Back off, buster," she said.

Fargo smiled as Evans came to an instant halt. "You've no right here," he said with considerably less aggressiveness.

"Finish your meeting. Then I want mine," Annie Dowd said.

Fargo fastened her with a narrowed glance. "You go home. I'll visit you there," he said.

She frowned and he knew she was thinking of demanding a promise, but she decided against the thought. "I'll be expecting," she said as she strode from the room, short, hard steps that gave her round rear a tiny wriggle.

Carol Siebert's voice brought his attention to her. "You're not really going to consider anything she says, are you?" the young woman asked with cool haughtiness.

"I'm going to listen to her," he said.

"You can't feel you owe anything to her?" Carol Siebert said.

"No, not to her," Fargo answered.

"Then to whom?" Carol frowned.

"To myself," he said, and saw the muted blue eyes study him for a long moment.

"An unexpected answer, I'll admit," she said. "It seems you have a streak of the knight-errant in you, Fargo."

"Whatever that means," he grunted.

"The need to help out young ladies in distress, even scruffy, unkempt little things," she said. "Commendable, but somewhat outmoded."

He smiled. The muted blue eyes were fascinating even when touched with reproach. "I'll try to remember that," he said. "Now I'll go listen to what she has to say."

"I must say, Fargo, I feel your first obligation is to us. We're the ones who sent for you and paid you to come," Evans said.

"I'll remember that, too," Fargo said as he walked from the inn. He climbed onto the Ovaro and rode into the heat of the afternoon sun, the damp, heavy air an invisible blanket. Sometimes he wished his prophecies weren't so often right, he told himself as

26

he thought about the perky-faced young woman. The worst kind, he grunted as he reached the place where he'd left her in the night. The land opened up and became a broad plateau dotted with palmetto trees and tupelos. He rode south and the house finally came into sight, flat-roofed, with a long barn stretching out from one side, almost a cow barn but too low.

Then he spied the hogs in a wide pen alongside, common stock but in good condition. However, the parade of fancy chickens that roamed freely were all special breeding stock, none of which he recognized. The small figure, a denim smock over he clothes and a feed pail in one hand, came out of the barn as he rode to a halt. She whipped the smock off and hurried to him, her high, round breasts bouncing under her shirt. "You raise pigs and fancy chickens," Fargo said as he dismounted.

"My folks did more of it before they died. I've cut down. It pays the bills," Annie Dowd said. "Most folks in this part of the state do small farming. There's no wealth around here and not much to do. That's why the families are so big."

"The oldest form of recreation," Fargo said. "But that has nothing to do with why you want to hire me."

"Only in a roundabout way," she said. "Young girls are being stolen from all over this area, right out from their homes, taken in the dead of night. Last month, my cousin Una was one of them."

"And you blame Max Garson," Fargo said.

"It happens whenever he shows up, every month or six weeks. I've taken a note of that, and last month I saw him poking around Una's home when she and her folks weren't there. I'm sure he's behind it."

"Nobody's been able to catch any of them or stop it?" Fargo questioned. "What about their families?"

"Some of the families have been killed. Others

never knew what happened until they found their daughter gone the next morning," Annie said.

"They're taken that quietly?" Fargo frowned.

"Yes."

"That's giving Garson a lot of credit. It doesn't seem to me that he and his men could be that smooth," Fargo said.

"He's not. I'm sure he's using others to do it."

"Others?"

"Seminoles," Annie said. "A little child said she saw Indians outside her house the night her sister was taken."

"I thought the Seminoles came to some sort of treaty with the army," Fargo said.

"Only a few of them. Many just disappeared deep into the Ocala and never came to peace with the government. Someone like Garson could be using them to get the girls. Then he takes them afterward."

Fargo frowned into space for a moment. It was not an impossible conjecture. The Seminoles were known for their stealth and craftiness. It was said that they could move like shadows, without sound or substance. He returned his eyes to Annie Dowd. "You want me to trail Garson and find your cousin," he said.

"Find her and put an end to Garson and his kidnapping of young girls," she said. "I told you, I'll better whatever they offer."

"It's not that simple," Fargo said.

"They're asking you to track down one man who went exploring for precious minerals. I'm asking you to put an end to this terrible slave trade in young girls. They want to be able to run their company. I want to save lives, dozens of lives now and to come," Annie Dowd said, and her brown eyes flashed righteous anger. He couldn't disagree with her, he realized.

"You've got your case and it's the best of the two, I'll give you that," he said. "But I wouldn't be here if they hadn't paid me to come down. I can't ignore that."

"You can't ignore this, either. One, you'll be going into the same unexplored country of the Ocala to look for Una as you will to look for Raynall. Two, I'll go along. I know more about that country than you do. Three, they didn't tell you that you're the fourth man they hired. They tried three trackers from around these parts," she said with a gleam of triumph in her eyes.

"You sure about that?" he questioned.

"Ask them. That's how I heard you were due here. They talked about getting in touch with you," Annie said, and then, with a hint of smugness, "The other three were never heard from again."

Fargo felt the stab of anger inside himself. There were many ways to lie and he didn't appreciate any of them. By omission was certainly one. "All right, Annie Dowd. I'll combine things, two for one. You pay half and they pay half," he said.

"Fair enough," she said with excitement quick in her voice.

"I'll go talk to them now," he said.

"What if they won't agree?"

"I think they will. I'll come by and tell you later," Fargo said, and climbed onto the Ovaro. He saw her watch him ride off, legs spread slightly apart, hips thrust forward, a scruffy, pugnacious little figure, completely unaware, he was certain, that she also exuded a rough-hewn, vibrant sexiness. He didn't hurry his way back to Snakebird and the inn.

George Evans showed his annoyed impatience as he rose from a chair in the lobby. "May I assume you found out there's nothing important that she wants you for," Evans said.

"Just the opposite, friend," Fargo said, and outlined Annie's need for him.

When he finished, Carol Siebert's muted blue eyes held polite disdain. "That is a distressing situation," she said. "However, I don't see that it affects our agreement for you to find James Raynall. It is an agreement, in my opinion."

"I came to listen. I did. That's no agreement, honey," he said.

"Are you saying you're considering her offer instead of ours?" Evans asked, protest in his voice.

"I'm saying I'll be going into the same territory for both of you. I'll combine the two," Fargo answered.

"Ridiculous. We want your full efforts on finding James Raynall," Carol Siebert said.

"One won't interfere with the other," Fargo said.

"We're not paying to share you with anyone or for you to bring along your own little bed-warmer," Carol said icily.

Fargo smiled. She could toss barbs, he noted. "You've sure as hell got her figured all wrong," he said.

"Maybe her, but not you," she snapped back.

He laughed this time. "One for you," he said. "But it won't be that way. You pay half, she pays half. You'll both get everything I can bring to the job. That's the deal, honey. Take it or leave it."

Carol returned a half-sneer. "Do we have much choice?"

"Well, you could go hire somebody else, the way you did three times before," he said evenly, and enjoyed the surprise that flooded all three of their faces. "I don't take kindly to being told half a story," he said, his voice hardening. "Anything else you've left out?"

"We didn't think that was important," Evans said, summoning a moment of bluster.

"We've different ideas of what's important. What else haven't you told me?" Fargo said.

"We'll give you everything we have when you're ready to leave," Evans said.

"Tomorrow morning, here, one hour after sunup," Fargo said, and Evans nodded. Fargo paused as he saw Carol Siebert's blue eyes still studying him.

"I'm not happy with it," she said. "I don't like dividing anything."

"Too bad," Fargo said evenly, and saw the color come into her cheeks as he strode away.

Outside, he swung onto the pinto and started back to Annie Dowd's place. The late-afternoon sun had dipped down the sky when he reached it. He found an elderly, white-haired man with a leathery face working beside her as she fixed a hole in the pen wire.

She halted at once as he appeared, and hurried to him. "This is Charley Reilly. He works the place with me; he'll be holding it together while I'm away."

Fargo exchanged nods with the older man as he saw the question hanging in Annie's flashing brown eyes. "They agreed," he said. "They didn't have much choice, as Carol Siebert put it." Annie dismissed the remark with a sniff. "We all meet at the inn one hour after sunup," he said.

"I'll be there," she said. "Will you stay and have some supper? Just beans and bacon, but I've got some soup with it."

"Why not?" he said, and she handed the pair of pliers in her hand to Charley Reilly.

"Finish up, will you, Charley?" she said, and the elderly man nodded. Annie Dowd turned toward the house and halted. Fargo followed her glance to where a row of six bottles were lined up atop a fence post. "I want to show you something, Fargo," she said. "You told me not to go around calling on men like Garson to draw on me. Maybe this'll put your mind at ease."

Fargo saw her hand go to the holster at her hip, a

surprisingly fast motion. The big Allen & Wheelock came out in her hand, a good, smooth motion, and she fired off six shots with accuracy and fair speed. Each of the bottles disappeared in a shower of glass leaving only the broken bottom glass stumps atop the rail. Fargo saw the smile of self-satisfaction come into her face as she looked at him and waited for his surprised accolade.

"Not at all bad," he said honestly.

"Not bad?" she flared, brown eyes flashing. "That was better than not bad. That was damn good."

"Good enough," he conceded. "But it doesn't change anything I said. There's always somebody faster. Don't ask for trouble."

"Somebody faster? I haven't found that," she sniffed smugly.

Fargo's hand flew to the Colt at his hip with the speed of a diamondback's strike and the revolver came out firing six shots with such speed they sounded as though there were but three. The small glass stumps of the broken bottles disappeared and the rail was suddenly bare. He lowered the Colt and turned to Annie. Her jaw hung open, her lips parted as she turned to him, brown eyes wide with astonishment. "You have now," he said quietly.

"Damn," she breathed. "I guess you made your point. But that was no ordinary shooting."

He reloaded the Colt and dropped it into the holster. "Just remember it," Fargo said, and she nodded.

"Let's go inside. That kind of shooting deserves some good Tennessee sippin' whiskey," she said.

He followed her into the house, where he found it more spacious and well-furnished than its outside appearance indicated.

Annie sat him in a stuffed chair, brought out a bottle of Tennessee sour mash and two glasses. The whiskey was warm and rich, with the particular flavor that only good sour mash possessed. She fixed supper while sipping from her glass, and he enjoyed watching her. She moved with a contained energy that held its own kind of gracefulness, everything held tightly together, the high round breasts dipping and turning as one, hips and legs moving with a quick, compact energy.

She refilled his glass as she put supper onto an oblong table.

"Better be careful. You know what you said about being nice to men," he slid at her.

She paused and he saw thoughts plainly tumbling through her as she gave him a long glance.

"You'd be different," she said.

"Spoken out of that vast knowledge you have about men?" he questioned blandly.

"Spoken out of what I feel inside. That's better than anything else," she said. He smiled, more to himself than to her. Inner wisdoms, he mused. He knew better than to deny them. "You'd be different," she said again, restating conclusions for herself.

The night descended as Annie sat across the table from him and the energy inside her came out again as she chattered on about her plans to add more fancy chickens until she became known as the place to go for special birds. He finished the whiskey with the last of the meal and helped her clean the plates.

"You sleep with your door latched?" he asked.

"Not usually, Charley's in his shack behind the barn. I feel safe," she said.

"Latch your door tonight and keep that six-gun beside you," Fargo said brusquely.

"Max Garson isn't going to come to steal me away," Annie said, and laughed at the thought. "He wants them younger, fourteen to eighteen."

"Wasn't thinking he'd come to take you, just to kill you," Fargo said. "You accused him of stealing the girls. If he is behind it, he'll want to shut you up," Fargo said.

"What do you mean, if?" Annie frowned. "You think I'm wrong?"

"Could be," Fargo said. "Getting close to the Seminoles would take a special kind of man. I can't see Garson doing it, much less getting them to steal girls for him. I can't see them obeying Garson for anything."

"It's got to be him. He shows up and there's another raid. It all fits," Annie insisted.

"If you're right, maybe we'd be smart not to leave in the morning. Maybe we ought to stick around and see what happens. If there's another raid, we'll be able to follow close on their heels," Fargo said.

Annie thought for a moment. "That's for you to decide," she said, and walked to the door of the house with him, her brown eyes grave. "Thanks," she said. "You didn't have to include me in."

"No, but I have to look in the mirror every morning," he answered.

"It's still thanks," Annie said. He heard her slip the inside bolt on the door as he rode into the warm night.

A cluster of tupelo trees rose some hundred yards from the house. He rode into their warm, fragrant silence, dismounted, and stretched out on the grass. If there was going to be a move against Annie, they'd wait till the night was deep. He closed his eyes and drew sleep around himself.

When his inner alarm went off, he snapped his eyes open to see that the moon was high in the midnight sky. He moved to where he sat down with his back against the deeply corrugated, dark-gray bark of a tupelo and let his eyes slowly scan the dark stillness. An hour passed when suddenly he saw the dark shapes come into sight, moving slowly, taking form as five horsemen. They spread out as they approached the house and barn, and he watched them halt, dismount, and move forward on foot. He pulled the big Sharps from its saddle case and left the trees, moving in a low crouch. The five figures were totally unaware of him as he drew closer. Their attention was focused on the house.

Two nearest the house came to a halt and Fargo peered through the night, a frown on his forehead. Suddenly a flare of flame erupted in the night and he saw that the two men had lighted a short torch. As the one drew his arm back to throw the burning torch against the house, Fargo took aim and fired. The man spun halfway around as the heavy bullet slammed into him. The torch flew almost straight up in the air and came down on the figure beside him.

"Jesus," Fargo heard the second figure scream as he was suddenly on fire, the tar from the torch splattering him with tongues of flame. He flung himself on the ground and tried to put out the flames by rolling and tumbling as he screamed in pain.

Fargo fired again and the man's screams stopped as he lay still. Some acts of mercy were planned, some not, Fargo told himself as he dived flat on the ground. The other three had turned and were spraying bullets in his direction. He lay prone, facedown, as two shots kicked up dirt too close. Holding the rifle against him, he rolled once, then again. He came onto his stomach once more with the Sharps in position to fire. His shot was a scant inch to the right of one of the three figures who fired from on one knee, and he saw the man fling himself sideways.

Annie was at the window now, he glimpsed, firing at the figures some few dozen feet from the house. But she was firing too fast and the light was bad. Her shots missed.

One of the men rose and started to race toward his horse. Fargo drew a bead on the running figure, fired, and the man pitched face-forward to lay still. A shot nicked the edge of Fargo's jacket and he rolled again, furiously this time, at least six turns before he halted and peered across the ground. The other two men were running now, one trying for the horses, but the last one almost at the cluster of tupelos. Fargo rose to one knee as Annie's shot missed the man racing for the horses and he ran forward in a long striding crouch, the rifle in one hand as he reached the edge of the trees. He heard the man crashing through the brush and he raced after him. But the night became nearly total blackness inside the tupelos, and he halted, listening, as he dropped to one knee.

The man had turned right and Fargo had to strain his ears to pick up the sounds of the fleeing footsteps. The semitropical underbrush had none of the crackle of the western brush. He listened to the soft, almost susurrant sound before moving after it. The cluster of tupelo ended soon and Fargo increased his pace in time to see the figure running from the trees across open land. He swore softly. He wanted the man alive to question, but the fleeing figure turned and twisted as he ran and the darkness made accurate shooting all but impossible. Yet he had to try. He halted, put the rifle to his shoulder, and aimed low. He fired and saw the man stumble and fall as he cursed in pain.

Fargo lowered the rifle and ran forward as the man lay on his side, one hand clutching his leg. "Don't do anything stupid. I just want some answers," Fargo called as he neared the figure. He had almost reached the man when he saw the figure half-turn and the six-gun come up in the man's hand.

Fargo flung himself sideways as the two shots hurtled past his head. He hit the ground, dropped his grip on the rifle, and yanked the Colt from its holster. The man, still on his side, fired again. The shot went wide. Fargo let two shots fly and saw the figure kick out stiffly, shudder, and lay still. Fargo rose, more carefully this time, approached the figure and holstered the Colt as he saw the man's staring eyes and red-stained chest.

He'd not be answering any questions. Fargo grimaced and turned, retrieved the rifle, trotted back to the cluster of tupelo, and finally emerged out on the front side of the trees.

Annie, a cotton nightshirt that barely reached her knees, stood beside her white-haired, elderly helper. She looked up as Fargo emerged from the trees. The torch still flickered on the ground beside two of the slain attackers. "You were right. They did come after me," she said, and came to stand close in front of him, high, round breasts pressing out the short nightgown. She had nicely formed calves, he noted, muscled yet graceful.

"Some of Garson's men," she said. "I recognize these two from the saloon."

"The other two also. One got away," he said. "Garson wasn't with them."

"I'll get the wagon, toss these critters inside, and take them to Jake Watson, come morning," Charley Reilly said.

Fargo walked back to the house with Annie. "There'll be no more trouble tonight," he said. "They tried and failed."

"Because you were waiting," Annie said, and her hand closed around his arm. "I'm real grateful to you. Once again," she added with a wry smile. She let her hand drop from his arm, a flash of sudden embarrassment in her perky face. "Sorry," she said. "I hate women who get all sticky."

"Nothing wrong with that," he said.

"And I don't want you to get the idea you need to be taking care of me," she said with firmness.

"Wouldn't think of it." Fargo smiled. "I'll think

some more about whether we ought to stay around or set out, come morning. You meet me at the inn ready to travel, just in case that's what I decide."

She nodded, her face grave. She closed the door as he strode away to where he had left the Ovaro. He rode slowly until he found a spot to bed down where the sweet scent of hyacinth drifted through the night. He had to decide on whether to leave or wait. The Raynall people would scream if he decided to wait. Not that he gave a damn about that. But if Annie was right about Garson, perhaps the man wouldn't strike this time, aware that he was perhaps being watched.

There'd be no fresh trail to follow, then, and he'd have let an already cold trail grow three days colder. He made a face as he pulled sleep around himself. Decisions could wait till morning.

3

He had pretty much decided to wait for a few days more when he reached the inn at Snakebird. Evans and Riggs were outside, waiting, and Fargo saw a brown mare carrying a full travel pack behind the saddle standing near Riggs. Carol Siebert rose from the other side of the mare where she had been adjusting the cinch strap, her tall, willowy figure clothed in tight-fitting riding britches and a white tailored shirt that all but molded itself around her breasts. She managed to look lovely, stylish, and efficient all at once.

"Going somewhere?" Fargo asked as a tiny stab of apprehension pushed at him.

"With you," Carol Siebert said, the muted blue eyes meeting his frown with cool calm.

"Hell you are," he growled.

"Hell I'm not."

"This is no damn tour."

"You're taking Annie Dowd," Carol said, her brows arching.

"Because she can help. She knows the Ocala."

"Yes, so you say," Carol replied with faint disdain.

"The only reason you want to go is to make sure you get your money's worth," Fargo said.

"No. I've other reasons to go, but now I have one more," Carol said coolly.

"What other reasons?"

"James Raynall listened to me. I could get him to

do things when no one else could," she said, and George Evans' voice cut in.

"That's right. He was very fond of Carol. If he's out there intent on exploring some find, Carol's the one person who can get him to come back or sign the papers she has with her. We had already decided she'd go along," the man said.

"I don't like it. I've no damn idea what we might run into." Fargo frowned.

"I'll take my chances," Carol said as she brushed a hand through her dusty-blonde hair.

"I'm not going to wet-nurse you, honey," Fargo said.

"Fine. I expect you've said the same thing to your scruffy little friend," she returned with a touch of waspishness.

"She won't need it," he snapped.

"Neither will I," Carol said, and he turned away as he saw the short-legged light bay, really a tan, come toward him with the small, wiry figure in the saddle.

Annie Dowd slid to the ground as she halted, brown hair brushed and shining, her face scrubbed and bright. "Don't look so surprised," she muttered as she met his eyes.

"You look right pretty," Fargo said, and she outwardly ignored the remark, though he knew she had taken it in. Her brown eyes flashed to Carol Siebert and the brown mare and back to Fargo.

"She's going with us," Fargo said.

"I'm not taking care of her," Annie growled.

"Nobody has to take care of me. I'm quite capable of doing that by myself," Carol Siebert snapped.

"Hah," Annie grunted.

"One doesn't have to be a half-wild ragamuffin to be capable," Carol hissed.

"Shut up, both of you," Fargo said. "Any more of

this and I'm on my way back to Wyoming." Carol tossed him a glance of cool tolerance as she fell silent.

Annie glowered. "We won't be needing to wait around," she said. "Zack Johnson came by this morning. His fifteen-year-old was stolen during the night. So were six other young girls, from here east to the St. John's River."

"Same method?" Fargo asked.

"Yep. All of them taken so quietly their folks never knew about it till they woke up this morning," Annie said.

"Mount up," Fargo said as he climbed onto the pinto.

Annie swung into the saddle and Carol exchanged last words with Evans and Riggs. When she finished, she rode up on his other side. He put the pinto into a trot as he left town and moved across a stretch of flat land. "How long to the Ocala?" he asked Annie.

"We ought to be there by noon," she said.

"What makes you think they take the girls that way?" he asked.

"Everything else around here is too open," Annie said, and he nodded at the answer and increased the pace some.

The day turned hot, steamy, and humid, a condition he had decided was normal down in this region, and he slowed the horses to a walk every ten minutes. Even so, after the second hour had passed and they rode alongside a small stream, Carol's tailored shirt was damp with perspiration as it outlined the tiny points on her full breasts.

"Can we rest?" she asked.

"Later. I've a trail to pick up first," he said, and saw Carol's quick glance at Annie.

"How come you're not perspiring?" She frowned at the other young woman.

"Half-wild ragamuffins don't perspire," Annie said tartly.

"The body makes its own accommodations when you live in a place," Fargo said, and both young women fell silent.

It was past noon when they reached the edge of the Ocala, the forest rising up in a towering combination of deep, dark greenness punctuated with brilliant floral colors. He halted and rested the horses just inside the cool shade and turned to Carol. "You said you had something to make this less of a wild-goose chase," he mentioned, and she fished a square of paper from her saddlebag.

"He left this. He said it was how he planned to start," she said.

Fargo frowned at the piece of paper. It was the crudest kind of map, little more than a series of scrawled marks and a few names lettered in. He showed it to Annie. "Mean anything to you?" he asked.

"One name, that one there," she said, pointing to a spot on the paper.

"Azard?" Fargo frowned.

"It's the name of a man who runs a stopping-off place and a trading post a ways into the forest," Annie said.

"A trading post in the middle of this place?" Fargo frowned. "What in hell for?"

"There are plenty of traders who come into the Ocala for gator hides, snakeskins, and egret plumes, to say nothing of deerskins. The Ocala is home to a big deer herd. Buyers go to Azard's, stay at his place while they make their deals. I heard some royalty has traveled there to buy things," Annie explained. "There are whole clans of backwoods families who supply Azard with the hides and skins he needs.

They're damn near wild people themselves, from what I've heard."

Fargo handed the square of paper back to Carol. "Maybe Raynall stopped there. It'll be a start," Fargo said. "And maybe Max Garson stopped there, too. Let's move."

Annie rode on one side of him, Carol on the other, as he began to push through the giant forest domain. The ground wouldn't show prints for more than an hour or two, he guessed, the weedy grass a springy blanket that quickly returned to its shape. Annie was right about the deer, he noted as he glimpsed white-tailed bucks almost everywhere he looked. The forest was also host to a plentiful water network, he noted as he glimpsed marshlands, swamps, lakes, and rivulets that dotted and crisscrossed the dense terrain. As they skirted the edge of one lake, he took in the towering cypresses that rose out of the water, each surrounded at the base by four to six gnarled pyramids of wood that also rose from the water.

"They have to be part of the root system," he said to Annie, and she nodded back.

"Folks call them knees. They're the breathing roots for each tree," she said.

Fargo's eyes scanned the forest as they rode. There was plenty of oak and laurel with some bluejack, and some other trees he knew: persimmon, buttonbush, the short saw palmetto, and the red maple. But there were many he didn't know and some that were a very major part of the forest growth. One, a tall tree with deeply corrugated bark and blue-black oblong berries almost an inch long, rose up to his left in clusters of increasing size.

"What's that tree?" he asked Annie.

"Cotton gum, part of the tupelo family," she said.

"And those nearby?" he asked, pointing to a cluster

of moderately tall trees with shiny, leathery leaves and dark-purple berries.

"Satinleaf," she said.

The next tree that caught his eye as they moved deeper into the forest was tall with smooth, thin, red-brown bark and clusters of whitish flowers flecked with green. "Gumbo-limbo," Annie said.

Another tree, which appeared singly, then in groups of twos and threes as they rode on, had a smooth, light-gray bark tinged with pink. It caught his eye and again he called on Annie. "Tamarind," she said. "I imagine we'll see more of those the deeper we go. They're a south Florida tree, I'm told." One thing became increasingly clear to him as he rode: You could get lost in any forest, but this one was made for it.

Perhaps it was the steamy, damp, closed-in feel of it. A dense, brooding air hung over it, and the foliage so overlapped itself that it seemed to become one trailless, encompassing mass. As they passed close to a marsh, he glimpsed two huge gray forms with hide not unlike armorplate slither into the water with surprising speed. Almost instantly, the two alligators lay still in the brackish water, only the tops of their long snouts and heads showing over the surface. To a hurried passerby they might have been two pieces of log. He sensed a little shiver from Carol on his right.

"Good God, they're ugly," she murmured.

"So ugly they're beautiful." Annie said, a touch of defensiveness in her voice. She plainly loved her land and all its creatures. Most of them, he corrected himself.

When darkness began to filter down through the dense foliage, he called a halt between two tall tupelos with a bed of springy grass between. His nostrils drew in the marshy odor in the air. The moon, when it rose, barely penetrated the foliage. The forest remained a dark, dank, and warm place. Annie and Carol had their own food in their packs and he ate some of the buffalo strips he carried in his.

Both were tired and offered no conversation, and that was fine with him. The resentment between them was still very much in the air. He needed no bedroll for the soft grass and the warmth, and he found a spot for himself alongside one of the trees and began to shed clothes. "Turn in. I'll want to be moving, come daybreak," he said, and saw Annie and Carol rise and move behind the trees. Modesty was unnecessary, he smiled. He could see little more than the dark outlines of their figures.

Both emerged in moments and settled down a few feet from each other. He wasn't sure, but he thought he detected Carol carrying a blanket as she lay down. He closed his eyes and listened to the night sounds. Some he knew, the cicadas, bullfrogs, horn beetles, click beetles, and the drone of flies and mosquitoes. But there were others he didn't know, sometimes a long, low, hissing sound, loud clicks, and the sound of claws scurrying up bark, too large to be a squirrel, too fast for possum. He finally drifted off to sleep to the strange, subdued cacophony of the forest that seemed half-jungle.

He woke with the dawn, which seeped its way through the green canopy and looked across at the two still-sleeping figures. Annie wore the short nightdress. It had crept up to reveal nice, solid thighs, full of youthful vigor that was its own kind of beauty. His eyes went to Carol. No blanket, he saw, but she had wrapped herself in a white sheet and only the dustyblond hair protruded. He walked some dozen feet from where they had camped and found a wide rivulet of water that ran into a marshy area. He washed and finished dressing.

Both young women were awake when he returned.

"Go past the purple and red flowers. There's water to wash in," he said.

Carol rose, the sheet wrapped tightly around her, took her clothes, and disappeared into the trees.

Annie, knees drawn up and the short nightdress pulled down, sat and gave the appearance of a rumpled gamin, her short, brown hair touseled atop her perky face. "You can concentrate on catching Max Garson," she said matter-of-factly.

"No favorites," Fargo said. "You'll each get the same attention."

"Favorites has nothing to do with it. We've a chance to catch Garson and put an end to him. She's on a wild-goose chase with no chance of success," Annie said.

"You can't be sure of that," he answered.

"Hell, the man's been gone almost two years. He's probably part of some swamp. And you know what, I don't think she gives a damn about finding him. She's just been sent to go through the motions so they can say they tried and go about reshuffling their company," Annie said. "I say spend your time trying to find what we've a chance to find."

"You both get equal treatment. That's the deal," Fargo said, though inwardly he couldn't deny Annie's logic.

She made a quick face and rose as Carol returned wearing a riding skirt and a shirt with short sleeves. She somehow managed to look as though she were out for a canter in a corral. Annie took her things and hurried away and Fargo watched Carol saddle the brown mare. Her eyes turned to him, cool amusement dancing in muted blue depths.

"Did she tell you not to waste time tracking James Raynall and concentrate on her objectives?" Carol asked, and Fargo knew the moment of surprise flashed in his face before he could stop it. Carol offered a smug little smile.

"How'd you know?" Fargo queried.

"I expected as much. She's probably never heard of the word 'ethics,' " Carol said, her patrician face clothed in cool disdain.

"She knows about caring," Fargo said, and realized he sounded defensive. "I mean, she's trying to do something good."

"Doing the wrong thing for the right reasons? Nice sentiments don't excuse unprincipled behavior. I guess it's a matter of how you're brought up," she sniffed.

"Maybe it's a matter of what you feel comes first, people or principles," Fargo said. Carol's smile was coolly dismissive. There was substance behind her hauteur and disdain, he allowed silently. They were different types, she and Annie Dowd, by nature and by environment.

"What did you answer, if that isn't too direct a question?" Carol said, her muted blue eyes waiting with private amusement.

"I told her a deal's a deal," Fargo said.

"At least you understand the word 'ethics,' " Carol said.

"I'll take any compliment, even a backhanded one," Fargo said, and caught the instant of embarrassment that flashed in her face. He broke off further conversation as Annie returned, hair brushed and looking freshly scrubbed. She swung onto the short-legged horse with her usual brisk pugnaciousness and he led the way south again.

The day quickly grew hot and the forest steamy as the land refused to offer up any semblance of a trail. Annie found a cache of papaya, which made a thirst-quenching and nourishing lunch. Carol's shirt was once again clinging to her, he saw as they rode on, and he was certain the flush of her face was not entirely due to heat.

It was midafternoon when he halted where two passages took form. One was a narrow passage into the depths of the forest, barely wide enough for riding single-file, a hot and humid place with vines and tendrils reaching out and hanging down. It was a dark and oppressive path that reached into the thickest part of the forest.

The other path bordered the edge of a narrow, oblong lake dotted with cypresses, a passage of easy riding and fresh air. Neither showed tracks of any kind. Fargo paused for a moment, then gestured to the dark, narrow, steamy passage.

"Wait," he heard Carol call. "Nobody would pick that way to go when they could take the path by the lake."

"Exactly what I'd want anyone following me to think if I were high-tailing it," Fargo said, and caught Annie's smile as he moved the horse into the dark, narrow trail. The forest engulfed him immediately, branches and vines reaching out and down to scrape against him, the thick air growing more humid and cloying almost at once. The fragrance of the subtropical flowers became the only redeeming feature of the narrow and winding path as he ducked his head to move under low, tangled branches. Annie was behind him, with Carol bringing up the rear. Brilliantly plumaged parrots were noisy moments of color as the passage grew still more narrow and he felt the pinto's hooves sink into soft ground.

They were surrounded by water—marshes, swamps, and lakes. He felt and smelled them more than saw them through the dense leaves. This was a forest that held as much water as it did land, he decided as he pushed his way onward. He held the slow steady pace for almost another two hours, and night was beginning to descend when he caught the glow of light through the dense foliage. He disregarded the vines and branches and put the Ovaro into a trot and heard Annie and Carol follow him, Carol giving less than ladylike sounds as she pushed through the branches.

The light grew brighter and became the wavering glow of kerosene lamps. The narrow passage ended with unexpected suddenness. He found himself in a small clearing, a long, low wood frame house in the center with six smaller frame cabins spreading out behind it. Four horses flicked their tails at a hitching post in front of the larger house, where lamps burned bright from inside. An almost illegible sign over the front door of the house read AZARD'S TRADING POST, and Fargo dropped the reins of the Ovaro over the hitching post. Annie and Carol came up to do the same as he swung to the ground. They followed on his heels as he entered the long, low building.

He stepped into a large room with gator and snake-skin hides piled to one side, four tables on the other, and a long bar and counter combined that faced the door. A tall man looked up from behind the counter as Fargo entered, his long face sharp and angular with a thin nose and prominent jaw, a black mustache matching very black eyes. Three men lounged with beer glasses at the counter, all medium height and all with sallow faces and narrow, mean eyes. One sported a handlebar mustache while the man next to him had a hollowed face darkened by a three-day stubble. The third, the youngest of the trio, looked at Annie and Carol with devouring intensity.

"You Azard?" Fargo asked the man behind the counter.

"That's right. Where'd you all come from out of the blue? I didn't expect nobody," Azard asked.

"Passing through. We heard you take in travelers," Fargo said.

"We do. Mostly buyers who come for skins. How'd you find us?" Azard said.

"Luck and a nose for finding things." Fargo smiled. "Then you can put us up for the night?"

Azard nodded and Fargo shot a quick glance at the other three men. He had them tabled at once as he saw the wolfish anticipation in their eyes as they looked at the two young women. Azard was the only one with brains enough to be curious.

"You say you're passing through, stranger? To where? There's no place here to pass through to," Azard asked.

"Going on south," Fargo said evenly. "Truth is we're on a search." He paused as Azard's brows lifted. "Two searches," Fargo added, and the man's brows stayed raised. "We're looking for a pack of jackals with seven young girls. Thought they might've stayed here last night."

"No, not here," Azard said, but Fargo's eyes went to the other three men and saw the quick glances they exchanged.

"Then, over a year ago, a man named Raynall was supposed to have come by here. You wouldn't remember him, would you?" Fargo asked, and Carol's voice cut in.

"Tall and handsome, grayish hair, straight nose, and a strong jaw, a man you can't meet without remembering," she said.

Azard shrugged. "Nope, he didn't pass this way," the man said.

"Too bad," Fargo said. "Where will we be bunking?"

"Any of the cabins out back," Azard said. "Pay in advance."

"Good enough," Fargo said. "We'll take two cabins."

Azard turned to the man with the stubble. "Open up cabins one and four for the folks," he said.

"One and four? Why so far apart?" Fargo asked mildly.

"They're our best cabins," Azard said as the stubble-faced man hurried from the room.

"Well, that makes sense," Fargo said pleasantly. "We'll get our gear." He strolled from the house with Annie and Carol, and Carol barely waited till they reached the horses.

"I'll take my own cabin, thank you," she said stiffly.

"You'll bunk together," Fargo said.

"There's no need for it. There are plenty of cabins," Carol insisted.

"Afraid you'll get fleas?" Annie snapped.

Carol's lips tightened, but she had the grace to half-apologize, Fargo noted. "No, I didn't mean anything like that," Carol said. "I just don't like doubling up, especially in this awful heat."

"You'll double up," Fargo said.

"Why, dammit?" Carol hissed.

"Because I can't watch two cabins, but I can keep an eye on one," Fargo said.

Carol's frown was real. "Don't you think we'll be safe here for the night?" she asked.

"Little Red Riding Hood," Annie sniffed.

"No, and I don't believe anything Azard said," Fargo answered. "I'm going to have a look around, come daybreak." The lamp went on in the nearest cabin and then in another at the other side of the semicircle.

The man hurried past them. "They're ready for you," he muttered with a quick glance at the two young women. As Annie went to get her things, Fargo stepped to the cabin and saw it was one large room with mattresses at each side and a broken-down dresser along one wall. A bucket of water rested in one corner, and Fargo's eyes went to the one window.

"Don't leave it more than a quarter open," he said.

"Oh, God, I'll die in this hothouse," Carol said. "And now you want to keep the window practically shut."

"One quarter open," Fargo repeated.

"I'm all hot and perspiry now, and I need a bath," Carol said.

"You can get one tomorrow."

"I'll never sleep a wink," Carol grumbled as Annie returned.

"Get your things and stop whining," Fargo snapped, and saw the muted blue eyes flare back.

"I'm not whining, dammit. I'm complaining. I want my own cabin," Carol snapped.

Fargo strode to the brown mare, took the pack from the horse, and tossed it at Carol's feet as she stepped from the cabin. He started to lead the Ovaro away when he found Annie beside him. "What are you planning?" she asked.

"To see that you two stay alive," he muttered.

"I know that. But how? You can't sit up all night watching and be fit to ride tomorrow," Annie said.

"That'll be my problem," he answered, and she half-shrugged, her hand closing around his arm.

"Thanks, Fargo. Again," she said, looking up at him, her pretty, perky face grave, the brown eyes darkened. He waited and saw the moment of hesitation in her eyes. Then she pulled her hand back and quickly turned toward the cabin, where Carol watched from the doorway. He waited till Annie closed the door before he walked to the other cabin. It was pretty much the same as the one with Annie and Carol, with a lone window. He couldn't see the other cabin from it, and he smiled grimly. That had been purposely arranged, of course, and he wondered if Azard often gave his three friends a chance for a little extra enjoyment.

Or perhaps the questions he had asked had triggered the rest. Fargo muttered a grim sound and turned the lamp off. The three lizards wouldn't move too soon. They had all night. They could afford to wait and be careful. He let perhaps a half-hour go by before he slipped from the cabin. The lamps were still lighted in the main house and he heard the murmur of voices as he moved toward the Ovaro in a half-crouch. The night was thick and hot. He took his lariat from the saddle strap and stayed in his long, loping half-crouch as he moved to the cabin where Annie and Carol were asleep. He smiled as he saw the window was not more than a quarter open. Moving around to the front of the cabin, he halted at the door, dropped to one knee, took one end of the lariat, and stretched it across the bottom of the door, not more than an inch from the ground. He tied the one end to a protruding piece of wood at the bottom of the cabin and stretched the rope taut as he moved from the doorway.

It was almost impossible to see in the darkness, he noted with satisfaction, and the trio wouldn't be looking for anything. He drew the lariat low to the ground as he moved around the cabin and found a spot under a cotton gum some fifty yards away. He lay down, the other end of the lariat wrapped around his wrist. When the cabin door opened, the bottom of it would hit against the rope and yank him awake. Meanwhile, he'd be able to get some sleep, he smiled, satisfied at his maneuver. He took a moment to cast a glance at the moon before he closed his eyes in the hot and sultry night.

When he woke, it wasn't with a tug at his wrist but with that sudden inner alarm that was as much a part of him as any outer sense. He sat bolt upright, his eyes sweeping the sky, and he instantly saw that the moon had moved down its trackless path. Three hours down, he estimated. Three hours without a tug at his wrist. Something was wrong. He swore silently as he rose and started toward the cabin in a low crouch. He saw the other end of the lariat still in place along the bottom of the door and swore again as he saw the window fully open. He dropped to one knee and strained his wild-creature hearing into the dark silence.

The sound came to him, hardly more than a murmur from beyond the tupelos that rose at the edge of the cleared area. He got to his feet, stayed in the low crouch as he ran and unwrapped the end of the lariat from around his wrist. He reached the trees, following the sound that had become low voices. Figures took shape in a glen where the moonlight streamed through a break in the overhanging foliage. Carol lay on the ground in a thin white nightgown. A gag covered her mouth and he saw she was unconscious. The three men were around her, one bending over her. The one with the handlebar mustache poked him on the shoulder. "Get some water and wake her up. You hit her too hard," he said.

"We didn't want her yelling, did we?" the other said as he rose.

"No, but we don't want to be screwing a dead fish, do we?" the mustached one said.

"Hell, no, I want her to know it." The younger one laughed in anticipation. The third one turned to hurry away and paused as Carol stirred.

Fargo crept closer and saw her eyes come open.

"Looks like we won't be needing any water," the taller one said as all three turned back to the young woman. Fargo saw Carol push herself up on her elbows, and the younger one pushed her down at once.

"Who'd do you want to give it to you first, baby?" He laughed.

Carol tried to twist free, but he was half atop her while the mustached one came around to pull her arms up. "Get the damn nightgown off her," the younger one said. They were absorbed with anticipation. None was aware of the powerful, silent shape that moved toward them on steps soft as a wolf's pads. Fargo had the Colt in one hand, but he didn't want gunshots. He didn't want Azard aware of a different turn to things. One of the trio was starting to yank the nightdress up and Fargo caught a glimpse of Carol's long, willowy legs as he reached the group. He brought the butt of the big Colt around in a sideways blow that smashed into the back of the youngest one's head.

The man fell to one side and Fargo's sweeping arc reached out farther and the Colt slammed into the second one's forehead as the man turned. He fell with his head spouting red. The tall, mustached one had time to fully turn, but surprise was still on his face. He lost a half-dozen precious seconds in staring at Fargo before he reached for his gun. His hand never touched the weapon as Fargo brought the Colt upward in a vicious uppercut and heard the man's jawbone break as the blow landed. The tall figure crumpled as though it were a rag doll suddenly emptied of all its stuffing.

Fargo turned to see that Carol had pushed to her feet and pulled the gag from her mouth. The thin nightgown clung to her long, willowy shape. Though she swallowed hard and there was still fear in her eyes, she somehow managed to seem quite composed. A built-in mask, he decided, perfected over the years. He cast a glance at the three figures. They'd be unconscious for a good while. "What'd they do with Annie?" he asked Carol.

"She's probably still in the cabin asleep," Carol said, and Fargo felt the frown dig into his brow.

"They didn't come in through the window and surprise you?" he asked.

He saw her suddenly look uncomfortable. "No, I

sneaked out through the window to sleep outside," she said. "It was too hot in there."

"Goddamn," Fargo bit out. "Why didn't you go out through the door?"

"I was going to, but Annie Dowd stopped me," Carol answered. "She said that you might be watching the door or that it might have something rigged up."

"So you went back and lay down?"

"For a while. But it was just too hot. I opened the window and climbed out to sleep outside on the grass," Carol said.

"Where they came onto you? Jesus, you can really be dumb, can't you?" Fargo snapped.

The muted blue eyes managed to flare. "I'm used to making decisions. Sometimes you make wrong ones," she said.

"That was sure one of them," Fargo growled.

"I'm sorry," she said, "and I'm very grateful that you came along." She covered her breasts with both arms, suddenly remembering she was clad only in the thin nightgown.

"Get back to the cabin," Fargo growled, and strode off as she hurried after him, his mouth a thin line and a grimness inside himself. He had underestimated little Annie Dowd. Carol had been more right about her than he'd let himself believe. He reached the cabin, gathered up the lariat, and yanked the door open. Annie sat up on the mattress and looked wide-eyed at him and Carol.

"What happened?" She frowned.

"Carol will fill you in. Meanwhile, I want to talk to you," Fargo said. "Outside."

Annie frowned, swung from the mattress, the short nightgown allowing him a flash of one sturdy thigh, but the material itself covered the rest of her with all modesty. She followed him outside; he walked a few dozen yards from the cabin, where he halted and spun around. He seized Annie by one arm and yanked her forward and saw the astonishment flood her face. "You really can be a little bitch, can't you?" he growled.

Her pert face continued to show only surprise. She could act, too, he grunted silently. "I don't know what you're talking about," she said.

"Like hell you don't. You let her go out that window."

"I'm a heavy sleeper. I didn't hear her," Annie said, her brown eyes growing narrow.

"Not that heavy. That old window had to scrape and creak when she opened it all the way. You just let her go out, and you knew they'd come onto her sleeping outside," Fargo said. "With her gone, I could concentrate on finding Garson."

Annie thrust her jaw forward. "I was fast asleep," she insisted.

"Bullshit, honey," Fargo said, and released his grip on her. "It seems Carol was right about you."

"Right about what?" Annie frowned.

"She said you never heard of the word 'ethics,' " Fargo told her. Annie made no reply, but her glower deepened. "Don't try anything like that again, you hear me?" he said.

"I didn't do anything," she muttered.

"You didn't, only in this case that was another way of doing something," Fargo returned harshly.

She spun on her heel, strode back to the cabin, and slammed the door shut.

Fargo returned to where he'd left the three men, and bound and gagged all three and pushed them into a cluster of tall sweetrush. He wanted Azard all to himself, come morning, and with a quick glance at the cabins, Fargo returned to where he had bedded down to finish out the remainder of the night.

4

Fargo woke with the first light, washed in a shallow, warm stream, and hurried to the cabins, where he began to examine each one, inside and outside. He was inside the fourth one when his glance caught a small, tortoiseshell object protruding from under one of the mattresses. He pulled it out and stared at it for a moment before slipping it into his pocket. He stepped from the cabin and saw that the long, low, trading-post house was still silent and closed. He strode to the cabin where Annie and Carol slept, to find Annie in the opened doorway. He saw Carol inside brushing her hair.

Annie faced him with the same glower she wore at the close of their last meeting. "I want to talk to you," she muttered.

"Later," he said, and held the tortoiseshell object out to her. "Found this in one of the cabins," he said.

Annie's eyes widened at once. "A hair clip. That's the kind Celia Jackson always wore," she gasped. "That means they were here. Azard lied."

Carol came to the door. "Maybe he lied about James Raynall, too," she offered.

"Wouldn't be surprised," Fargo said. "You two stay here. I'm going to get the truth out of Azard." He turned and strode away. When he reached the long building, he saw the tall, angular-faced man opening the front doors of the building. Azard was in only trousers and moccasins, but he had his six-gun strapped on, Fargo noted.

"You're up early, mister," Azard said.

"Didn't sleep well. There was trouble last night," Fargo said.

"Trouble?" Azard said, and let himself appear surprised. "I didn't hear anything, but then I'm a heavy sleeper. What kind of trouble?"

"Those three lizards of yours tried to attack one of the young women with me," Fargo said evenly, and watched Azard let surprise turn to astonishment in his face.

"No," the man said.

"You're real shocked, of course," Fargo said.

"I sure am. I'll see that they pay for that, mister," Azard said.

"That's been taken care of," Fargo said, and saw the moment of alarm slip over the man's face.

"What's that mean, mister?" Azard asked with a frown.

"It means they're not dead," Fargo said. "But you will be unless I get some straight answers."

Azard's face stiffened. "Don't threaten me, mister," he growled.

"No threat. Just stating facts," Fargo said evenly.

Azard gave a half-shrug and let his face relax. "No need for trouble. I'm a peaceable man," he said, and seemed to start to turn away. But Fargo's eyes were on the man's hand, ready to seize that split-second advantage that could spell the difference between life and death. It came in the tightening of the man's fingers, his wrist muscles contracting as Azard went for his gun. But the Colt was already in Fargo's hands and firing, a single shot. Azard cursed in surprise and pain as the six-gun flew from his fingers. Fargo had hit the revolver butt with deadly accuracy and Azard shook his momentarily numbed hand in pain.

"Mistake number one," Fargo said. "You don't get a second." Fargo saw Annie and Carol run from around the cabin at the sound of the shot. They came to a halt as they saw him and Azard. "Thought I told you two to stay put," Fargo said without taking his eyes from Azard.

"Maybe you expect too much," he heard Carol return. He made no reply as, his eyes still on Azard, he beckoned the man out of the doorway. His lake-blue eyes, now as cold as an ice floe in January, bored into Azard, who still shook his hand.

"I'm already feeling irritable, cousin. That means I'm low on patience and time. Now, for every bullshit answer I'm going to shoot off a piece of you," he said, and the man glared back. "Garson was here with the girls. How many men did he have with him?" Fargo questioned.

"I don't know what you're talking about," Azard rasped.

The Colt barked and Azard's hand flew to the side of his head, where the top of his ear had disappeared. "Owooo, Jesus," the man cried out. "You son of a bitch," he flung at Fargo.

"How many men did he have with him?" Fargo asked.

"Go to hell," Azard shouted. The Colt exploded again and this time Azard's other hand flew to the side of his face, where the top of his other ear spouted red. "Oh, goddamn, Jesus . . ." he half-screamed in pain.

Fargo's eyes narrowed in thought. Azard wasn't the kind for being a martyr or loyal. He was afraid Garson would return. Which meant the place was a regular stop for him. Fargo swore silently. He had no choice but to make fear of the moment greater than fear of the future, to make pain overcome prudence. "How many, Azard?" he growled. The man flung another curse, and this time Fargo's shot blew his large toe off.

Azard screamed in pain as he dropped to the ground, held his bleeding foot out, and Fargo fired again, grazing his heel. He saw fear in Azard's eyes for the first time. He reloaded, dropped five shells into the chamber of the Colt, and started to bring the weapon up as Azard watched with increasing horror in his face. "Just him and the goddamn Indians," Azard blurted out.

"Indians?" Fargo frowned.

"The Seminoles. Four of them," Azard said, and groaned in pain as he moved his foot.

Fargo felt the frown digging into his forehead. "Four Seminoles with Garson," he repeated, and Azard snapped out an answer out of pain-filled anger.

"That's what I said, goddammit," the man said.

"Garson, four Seminoles, and the girls," Annie's voice cut in.

"Two girls," Azard said.

Annie's eyes went to Fargo. "He's lying again. There were seven girls taken," she said. Fargo raised the Colt again and instant horror swept Azard's face.

"No, goddammit. Two girls. That's all they had with them, two," the man almost screamed. Azard wasn't lying. There was too much real fear in his face, and Fargo lowered the gun a fraction as he tossed another glance at Annie.

"That doesn't figure. He's lying. I know seven girls were taken," she said.

Fargo's eyes were narrowed as he answered, "No, he's not lying, but I think we just learned something about how Garson does it," Fargo said to Annie. "He splits his people into at least three groups. That's how they hit different places at the same time. Then they take off with the girls they've taken and go back to wherever it is they go by different routes."

"Yes, of course." Annie nodded as she took in his explanation. "But I was right about him using the Seminoles."

"It sure looks that way, but I still don't understand it. He's just not the kind of man they'd work for. It just doesn't figure," Fargo said.

"They're doing it, whether it figures or not," Annie returned, and he had no answer.

"What about James Raynall?" Carol's voice cut in, and Fargo turned to Azard. The man had pulled his shirt off and was wrapping it around his foot.

"You heard the lady," Fargo rasped.

"I don't remember everybody that stops here," Azard barked.

"You don't have that many people," Carol said, and then, to Fargo, "He's lying again. I just know it."

She was probably right, Fargo agreed. It was worth a try. He lifted the big Colt and this time the barrel of the gun pointed straight at Azard's chest. "I'm tired of your lying. You're getting to be a damn bore," he said. "You're not worth staying alive." He pulled the hammer back and watched the terror flood Azard's face.

"No, Jesus, I remember now. He was here," the man blurted out. "He was here."

"It's amazing how the memory comes back," Fargo said. "Remember some more."

"He stayed for almost two months," Azard said.

"Doing what?" Fargo pressed.

"He'd go out into the Ocala each day and come back with pieces of soil. He had some fancy instruments in his bags. He'd ask questions of everyone who stopped by," Azard said.

Fargo's glance went to Carol. "That sounds right." She nodded.

"Keep remembering," Fargo rasped at Azard.

"That's all there was. He got to be a pain in the

ass, but his money was good and he finally took his gear and left," the man answered.

"Left to where?"

"South, straight into the trees. He said he was going to go deeper into the Ocala than any white man had been," Azard said. "He was a strange one, he was."

Fargo holstered the Colt and turned away. "Let's go. Get your horses," he said to the two young women as he strode to the Ovaro. He glanced back to see Azard limping his way into the house as they rode away. He'd look for the three others after he tended to his own wounds, but none would be pursuing, Fargo was certain. He turned south through the thick forest and set a slow pace in the steamy heat.

Carol called out before a half-hour had gone by. "Can we rest some? I didn't sleep any last night," she said. "Even a short rest would help."

Fargo nodded and found a spot between two laurel oak and a tall cotton gum where a half-circle of soft grass beckoned. Carol slid from the brown mare, stretched out on the grass, and closed her eyes. She was asleep instantly and Fargo glanced at Annie.

"You said you wanted to talk to me. This seems a good time," he said. She nodded and he followed as she strode into the trees away from Carol's sleeping form. She faced him, her face grave, brown eyes deep and dark.

"You were right about last night," she muttered. "I heard her go out the window."

Fargo's eyes searched her pert countenance, contrition wreathing her face. "Why the confession?" he asked.

"I've never been a liar. I figure this is no time to start, especially with you. You don't deserve lies, what with the things you've done for me," Annie said.

"You didn't feel that way last night. Why?" Fargo pushed at her.

She made a face. "I was afraid of what you'd think of me if I admitted it," she said, and he peered hard at her. No deceit in the brown eyes, he decided, only shame. "I won't do it again," she added, and he kept his face impassive. "I know what you're thinking. I can't blame you," Annie said.

"And what is it I'm thinking?" Fargo queried.

"That talk's cheap," Annie said.

He smiled inwardly. He could offer forgiveness, but she was a little hard-nose that deserved to be contrite. He'd let her stew a while longer, he decided. "We'll see," he said, and then, more gently, "But I'm glad you told me."

"Me, too," Annie said with a quick half-smile. She walked close beside him as he returned to the little clearing. Carol was sitting up, her muted blue eyes narrowed at him as he returned with Annie.

"I'm too hot and sticky to sleep. I need a bath. Find us some water," Carol said.

"Shouldn't be too hard." Fargo nodded and pulled himself into the saddle.

Carol followed, with Annie drawing up in the rear as he entered a narrow passageway. He rode some fifteen minutes when he spied the wild celery and turned the Ovaro to the left to follow the plants. The water appeared minutes later—a small lake, musk-grass plentiful along one section of the nearest bank, but the water clear nearby. Fargo halted, his eyes sweeping the shore, where tree roots seemed to tumble in careless profusion into the water.

He halted and turned to a half-circle of clear land, the small lake visible through the tupelo and sour gum.

Carol slid from the mare, rummaged in her pack, and brought out a towel. "May I go first?" she asked, the question polite but her tone one of faintly imperious expectation.

Annie shrugged her consent but her glance went to Fargo and he caught the message in her eyes.

"I'll go along with you," he said to Carol.

The muted blue eyes turned on him with cool amusement. "I don't want an audience," she said. "I'll expect you to be a gentleman and stay here."

"My being a gentleman could cost you your ass," Fargo said.

Carol's eyes flicked through the trees. "It's a perfectly peaceful little lake," she said, and returned her eyes to him. "But as it's my ass, as you so delicately put it, I'll take responsibility for it."

"I've got a conscience," Fargo growled.

"Nice try." She smiled. "I'm sure there's room for one more thing on your conscience."

He shrugged and Carol strode off toward the lake, moving quickly through the trees, and his eyes went to Annie. She read the question in his eyes as she shrugged. "Nobody knows how long they can stay underwater, not really. I've heard a half-hour, an hour. Nobody really knows," she said.

"Damn," Fargo bit out.

Annie's smile was wry. "You've a problem, it seems. You go after her and nothing happens, you're a no-good Peeping Tom. You don't go and something happens, and it's your fault."

"I don't need it spelled out, honey," Fargo said grimly.

Annie strode to the Ovaro and pulled the big Sharps from its saddle case. She strode away through the trees as she tossed words back at him over her shoulder. "She won't even know I'm there," she said.

He leaned back against one of the oaks and waited, letting himself enjoy the beauty of the parrots that swooped in unexpected bursts of color. Finally he spotted the movement through the trees and Annie appeared and handed him the rifle. "She's finished,"

Annie said, and a few minutes after Carol appeared looking refreshed and quietly lovely, her dusty-blond hair brushed back loosely.

"No problems. Aren't you glad you decided to be a gentleman?" Carol asked with a touch of sarcasm in her tone.

Annie's voice cut in. "You want to do me?" she asked, and Fargo nodded. "Give me a three-minute start," Annie said, and hurried into the trees.

Carol watched her go with one brow arched. "My goodness. It seems we have a little exhibitionist with us," she said.

"What we have is a little bitch," Fargo growled, and Carol's head swiveled and the muted blue eyes grew darker. "A big gator can stay underwater a long time before it surfaces," Fargo said. "I'll be there just in case."

Carol's face stiffened. "You mean, I really might have been in danger?" she asked.

"Annie was watching. She had the rifle with her," Fargo said, and brushed past her as he strode into the woods. But he saw the flush of color rise up from her long neck to flood her cheeks. He hurried, pushed through hanging vines, and reached the edge of the lake where Annie's clothes were strewn. She was in the water and waved a hand to him. His eyes swept the shoreline for any sign of movement, then scanned the surface of the lake, but there was only Annie rippling the water.

He smiled as she played, dived, surfaced, turned, and dived again, all the while never letting anything but her head, shoulders, and arms show abovewater. She reminded him of an otter as she turned and twisted, each movement fluid and graceful and all the while keeping modestly below the surface. Modestly and with mischievous tantalization, he decided. She knew he watched and she plainly enjoyed her little performance. But finally she halted and swam toward him, halting some six feet from the shore, treading water as she looked up at him. "Thanks," she said simply.

"Does that mean I should leave?" he asked blandly.

"It does," she said.

"What if I don't want to?" he returned.

"You went along with being a gentleman for Miss Uppity. You saying I'm different?" Annie thrust back, instantly belligerent.

"No, simmer down, you damn little hellcat." He laughed. "Maybe I just didn't fancy seeing her in the altogether."

"Like hell." Annie frowned. "She's damn good-looking. I'll give her that. You wouldn't be turning your back on her."

"Get out of that water so's I can get some grime off," Fargo said, and he turned his back as Annie came ashore. She called to him when she finished, and he turned to see her dressed, gun belt on, and her touseled hair brushed back, a pert little gamin and prickly as a cactus.

"I'll stand watch for you," she said, and he handed the rifle to her and began to shed clothes as he walked to the edge of the water. He saw her turn her back until he was in the lake and he smiled. She was a funny little mixture of hard and soft, brass bold and little-girl shy. He dived, let the water wash the road dirt from his powerful frame, swam leisurely and enjoyed the warm water. When he finished, he swam to the shoreline, rose from water and Annie quickly turned away.

"I'll borrow your towel," he said, and she nodded. When he was dried and dressed, he took the rifle from her and she walked close beside him as they returned to the half-circle. Carol's eyes held a faint touch of amusement as she watched Annie hurrying to keep up with Fargo's long strides. Fargo paused as he saw that Carol had rolled the bottom of her blouse up to form a bare midriff garment.

"You're smartening up," he said as he put the rifle into its saddle holster.

"It's so damn hot in this place," Carol said. The blouse, pulled tight as it was rolled up, outlined the lovely slow curve of her breasts while the bare midriff accentuated the narrowness of her waist. Fargo checked the saddle on the Ovaro and loosened the cinch strap a notch and saw Carol turn to Annie. "It seems I owe you a thank-you," she said. "I didn't know you were standing guard while I was in the lake. That was very nice of you."

Fargo saw the surprise in Annie's face turn to embarrassment. She was plainly not used to accepting thanks. "You didn't understand. Somebody had to go watch," she muttered.

"It was still very gracious. I do thank you," Carol said. Fargo's eyes narrowed at her. She was sincere, he decided. She couldn't keep the faintly patronizing quality from her voice, apparently. But Annie hadn't caught it and he pulled himself into the saddle. "I'll follow behind," Carol said. "I'm still awfully tired."

He nodded and began to move on again, Annie swinging in beside him. She waited till Carol had fallen back some dozen yards, her dusty-blond head nodding as she rode. "Why'd you tell her?" Annie hissed at him.

"It came up," Fargo said. "And she thanked you. That was the right thing to do." Annie uttered a derisive little snort. "Don't be so damn peppery. Learn how to accept thanks," Fargo said.

"It was only because of you," Annie sniffed.

"No, it wasn't. She meant it. I didn't tell her to say a damn thing."

"Maybe not, but it was still because of you."

"What's that supposed to mean?" Fargo frowned.

"She knew what you'd think if she didn't thank me, and she didn't want that," Annie said.

"Damn, I didn't think you were that bitchy," Fargo said with honest surprise.

"I'm not bitchy. I'm just saying it the way it is. She's taken a real shine to you," Annie said.

Fargo laughed softly. "That's crazy," he said. "She depends on me now. That's all it is."

"It's more than that. I've seen the way she looks at you when you don't know it," Annie said.

Fargo shook his head in mild exasperation. "Of course, you're such an expert on men and women. You've had so much experience," he pushed at her.

Annie remained adamant, her pert face set. "You don't need a hell of a lot of experience to know when a sow's looking to get bred," she said.

"I'm sure Carol would enjoy that little comparison," he commented blandly.

"You wait and see," Annie snapped, and fell silent as they rode on.

Fargo turned to glance back at Carol. She had come awake and rode slowly but with cool composure. Annie's thoughts were way off-target, he was certain. He'd never caught anything but cool, slightly patronizing composure on Carol Siebert's part. Yet the muted blue eyes were their own kind of mask. He turned away and amused himself with the possibilities that might lurk behind the shaded orbs. The speculation helped pass the time as the day grew hotter and the forest steamier. He finally called a halt alongside a line of sour gum.

"We'll rest a spell and let the sun go down some," he said as he dismounted.

Carol sank to the grass at once and was asleep in moments, lying on her side as one cream-colored breast edged over the neckline of her shirt in a long, lovely curve.

Annie napped sitting up against a tree, arms folded across her drawn-up knees, and somehow managed to exude pugnaciousness even asleep.

Fargo stretched out, listened to the forest sounds, and napped until the sun was no longer directly overhead. When he woke Annie and Carol and led the way on, he held to a slow pace and swore softly at the absence of even one set of tracks.

He continued to move south through the forest as the foliage grew thicker and passages became narrower. Swamps, marshes, and lakes continued to dot the denseness, appearing sometimes as if by magic. Carol continued to ride a half-dozen paces behind, and he caught Annie's glance on him as the day wore on, a question in its frown. "Ask," Fargo grunted, and she let a moment of embarrassment cross her pert face.

"I'm sorry, but I just couldn't help wondering," she said. "You seem to have stopped looking for tracks."

"Think I'm getting discouraged and giving up?" He laughed.

"I wouldn't blame you," Annie said. "We don't seem to be finding anything to follow."

"First, it's too soon to give up. Second, I can spot tracks almost without looking for them. Comes with experience," he told her.

"I'm sorry. Apologies," she said.

"No, you're paying. It's your right to ask and you're half-right," he said. "This damn grass is too flat and springy. I'm watching for broken branches, young shoots snapped off by horses brushing past, vines and leaves bruised and pushed back." She nodded, and he thought he saw a tinge of admiration in her brown eyes. He pushed through a narrow pathway that appeared and stayed with it as it went deep into the heavy forest. The day was beginning to near an end when he called a halt where the passage widened and Annie let out a little gasp of delight.

"Look, cocoplums," she said, and pointed to the top of a tree that grew some fourteen feet high, a small member of the towering trees of the Ocala. He followed her gaze and saw that upper branches were full of pink fruits about the size of small apples. Two more trees of the same kind grew alongside it and Annie swung to the ground and started for the tree. "I'm going to climb up and get some," she said. "Cocoplums are juicy and tasty. They'll go well with our beef strips."

He shrugged, dismounted, unsaddled the Ovaro, and watched Annie as she pulled her way up to the upper branches of the tree. Carol had come to stand near him as she watched, and suddenly he saw Annie's wiry form seem to freeze in place. He peered at her and saw her clinging to the branch, unmoving, as if suddenly carved in stone. Carol exchanged a glance with him and he called out softly, "Annie?" But Annie didn't move, not a finger, not a muscle. Fargo felt the frown deepening in his brow. He moved his gaze slowly across the branches alongside her and heard the sharp intake of his own breath. His eyes held on a long, slender form that lay half-wrapped around the branch only some eight or nine inches from Annie, its brilliant red, yellow, and black rings marking it as a coral snake, perhaps the most deadly of all American venomous serpents.

Fargo saw the snake's tongue flick out to test the air and draw in sensations. His eyes returned to Annie. She was in a position to reach her gun. She was a crack shot, he knew, remembering the little demonstration she had put on for him. All she had to do was move very slowly and carefully. The snake was not ready to strike. But Annie remained absolutely motionless and his frown deepened. She wasn't being extra careful and Carol's whispered words echoed the realization that flooded through him.

"She's frozen. She can't move," Carol murmured.

Fargo caught the movement from the other branch. The coral snake had begun to slide forward. Fargo whipped the Colt from its holster and dropped to one knee. He used his other hand to steady himself. He'd have but one shot, he realized, and brought the black-and-yellow head of the snake into his sights. His finger pressed slowly against the trigger. Split seconds suddenly seemed like minutes and then the pistol fired, the shot shattering the stillness. He saw the snake's head explode and the rest of its brilliant body thrash against the branches in a reflex action.

His eyes went to Annie as she fell, her head back, dropping straight through the tree, bouncing from one branch to another. He ran forward and reached the bottom of the tree in time to catch her before she hit the ground. He lowered her compact body to the ground as Carol came up.

"She's out cold. She fainted," Fargo said as he carefully moved each of Annie's arms, then her legs, and gently moved her head from side to side. "Nothing broken. Probably because she was limp as she fell and the branches were close enough so she never went into a long drop," he said. He started to rise to get his canteen when he heard the soft moan and dropped back to one knee beside Annie.

Her eyes fluttered, finally pulled open, and she stared blankly at him. "You're all right," he said, and saw the deep-brown eyes begin to focus.

"Oh, God," Annie murmured and tried to sit up, and he helped her. She clung to him for a long moment and then pulled away, embarrassment flooding her face. "It always happens, snakes and me," she said. "They terrify me. I freeze up when I'm close to one. I can't help it. I can get hold of myself if there's some space between us, but up close I just freeze. Then I faint. I feel like such a damn fool."

"It's over, relax," Fargo said, and her hand closed around his arm.

"I don't blame you if you don't understand. I don't really, myself. It just happens. A visiting doc once told me snakes have that effect on some people, maybe because of something that happened when they were very little. They don't know."

He felt the shiver go through her and she leaned against him, not at all her usual independent, peppery self. "I don't have to understand. There are a lot of things I don't understand," Fargo said. "It all came out all right. That's all that matters."

"Thanks to your shooting," Annie said, still clinging to him and then pulling away. "I'll be all right soon as I sleep some. That's the way it always is. It leaves me feeling emptied."

He nodded and pulled her to her feet and walked her to a spot where a bed of soft spineleaf moss formed a small circle. She sank down and her eyes were closed in seconds.

Fargo walked back to where Carol waited as night fell. "The world is full of surprises," he muttered.

"So I've heard," Carol said as the pale moon filtered down, allowing just enough light to find the horses and the beef strips inside saddlebags. Carol sat beside him as he chewed the food and his glance moved to Annie as she slept, a small, silent mound of darkness. He heard Carol's voice, but it took him a moment for her words to register. He turned, frowning, to peer at her.

"Did I hear you right?" he questioned.

"You did. She wants you," Carol said. "Little Annie wants you."

"You sure are reading that all wrong, honey,"

Fargo said, and almost laughed. "Annie Dowd doesn't take to men, not in that way. She's got a real thorny attitude on men."

"She takes to you," Carol insisted.

"She's just grateful. That's all there is to it. She's not the average woman, believe me," Fargo answered.

"She's a woman, average or not, and she wants you. Maybe she doesn't even know it herself, but she does," Carol said. "Another woman always knows." With that adamant remark, Carol rose and took her things from her pack and stepped into the trees. When she reappeared, Fargo caught the soft sound of the silk nightgown as she lay down on a sheet.

He rose and began to undress to almost nothing in the hot night with its faintly sweet, floral scent. He glanced at Carol and saw she had turned on her side and watched as he shed clothes. Not that she could see much in the darkness, he was certain. Perhaps she was letting imagination fill in for vision.

He lay down, stretched, and put his hands behind his head and thought about what Carol had insisted. Now each had said that the other wanted him. Why? he wondered. Were they so suspicious of each other that they misread every ordinary gesture? Or were they each taking the same way to tell him they'd be watching to be sure he didn't play favorites? Both were possible, and he felt the smile touch his lips. There was another possibility. What if they were both right? The thought intrigued even as he wanted to reject it. He'd picked up no signs on his own. But then he was sometimes fooled. Not often, yet it happened. He decided not to reject the thought, merely to set it aside and enjoy its intriguing promise.

He turned on his side and let the hot fragrant air bring sleep.

5

Fargo woke with the new day and saw Annie emerging from the trees, dressed and scrubbed. She halted and turned her back but not before she took in the muscled symmetry of his body.

"Go on and dress. I'll wait," she said, and he pulled on trousers.

"You can turn around," he muttered, and she turned and he saw the night's embarrassment still stayed in her face.

"I feel such a damn fool," she hissed.

"Forget it," he told her.

"I hate myself. I feel like one of those damn women who are always fainting at the drop of a hat," she said. "I'm not one of those, dammit."

"I know that," he said, and a moment of gratefulness touched the deep-brown eyes. "So why don't you get us those cocoplums for breakfast while I finish dressing," he said, and she whirled and headed for the tree.

It was what she wanted and needed to do and he'd given her the excuse, he realized. Besides, it was damn unlikely there'd be another snake up the tree.

He saw Carol wake and sit up, quickly wrapping the sheet around herself as she pushed to her feet. She stretched and the sheet slipped to her waist and she shook her dusty-blond hair. She looked beautifully willowy, her strong shoulders bared, the nightgown clinging to the long line of her breasts. She took her clothes from the brown mare and disappeared into the thick foliage.

She returned wearing the blouse tucked up bare-midriff again just as Annie scrambled down from the tree, her pockets filled with the fruit, which turned out to have a sweet, fresh flavor. When they finished breakfasting, he led the way on through the narrow path that remained narrow with a profusion of branches, vines, and hanging tendrils all combining to make it a claustrophobic place. It was only when the day began to wind down that the passage began to widen and the foliage became less oppressive.

Moving very slowly, Fargo caught sight of water ahead and to the left. He reined to a halt as a frown dug into his brow, and he strained his ears toward the water. He caught the sound again, faint but unmistakably voices, and he motioned for silence to Carol and Annie. They swung from their saddles as he slid from the Ovaro.

"Leave the horses here," he whispered, and began to move through the trees toward the water that took shape as a sizable lake. The voices sounded again, clearer this time, and he dropped into a crouch as he moved closer to the river. The tree cover was plenty thick, mostly laurel oak and cotton gum but becoming heavy with cypress as he neared the water.

He paused as his nostrils drew in a new odor—wood smoke and the scent of fish being cooked. He dropped to one knee and motioned for Annie and Carol to do the same as the voices came again, near and clear now. As he watched, a small boat moved into sight not far from the shore of the lake. A boxy little craft, kind of a crude rowboat with no real prow, it held three youngsters, two girls and a boy, all some ten to twelve years of age, he guessed. One girl wore a ragged, torn, one-piece dress, the other was clad only in a skirt, small, immature breasts deeply tanned. The boy wore only torn trousers cut off at the knee. All three had long, uncombed brown hair, and while the boy poled the little craft through the water, the two girls trailed nets behind it.

When they floated out of sight, Fargo rose and moved forward again. As he drew closer to the shore, he heard the distant murmur of voices, and when he reached the edge of the trees, he dropped to one knee again and found Carol and Annie alongside him. His eyes went to where the lake curved, the shore clear back some twenty yards and a village spread along the water's edge. He took in a dozen buildings, most little more than ramshackle huts, many with thatched roofs. A few of the structures were a little more substantial, wood-roofed with logs forming the sides.

The shoreline was dotted with small boats, a few rowboats, others larger versions of the snub-nosed craft that had passed him, and a few that seemed almost pirogues out of the Louisiana bayous. Large nets and ropes were coiled near the boats. His eyes moved into the village again.

Open cooking pits lined one section with meat-drying racks nearby. Men, women, and children were scattered through the forest village, the men for the most part with beards, clad in overalls, many without shirts. The women wore hand-sewn one-piece garments, shapeless and threadbare, many hardly covering up their naked bodies underneath. He noted a number of boys and girls in their early youth, between twelve and sixteen, he guessed. The boys wore knee-length pants, the girls were either in short garments that showed young, sturdy legs or clad only in skirts that showed smallish but firm, high breasts that hardly bounced as they ran and played.

Fargo's gaze moved slowly across the village once again, this time noting hunting bows along with rifles leaning against almost every shack. Some of the rifles were old .45 long-barreled Kentucky sharpshooter muskets, and he saw a number of old plains rifles along with a few long muzzle-loaders. Some of the men carried revolvers in holsters slung low on the hip, but these men were mostly rifle-shooters, it was obvious. A movement in the water drew his eyes a few feet from the shore and he saw three big alligators surface and swim lazily past the village to disappear underwater again.

Annie's voice was a whisper at his elbow. "The forest people," she said, awe in her voice. "I've heard stories about them. Everybody has, but very few people have ever seen them."

"What kind of stories?" Fargo asked.

"Stories about how they kill strangers and about how they're wilder than any Indian tribe," she said. "I've heard that the first of them, a long time ago, were from a prison ship that was wrecked off the coast with both men and women aboard."

"What else have you heard?" Fargo questioned as he took in bets and ropes curled near the boats at the shoreline. They were well-kept and in good condition. Obviously, the forest people lived by fishing, hunting, and trapping.

"I've heard they don't like strangers and they take captives," Annie said. "They share their womenfolk and everybody initiates a young girl the minute she's old enough. They bring hides to Azard, I've heard, in exchange for liquor, and they hold drunken rites to the moon."

"They speak English. I can hear them," Carol cut in. "Stories are like rumor. They're always exaggerated. I'll bet they're nothing more than backwoods people, inbred and isolated and more afraid of strangers than anything else."

Fargo's eyes moved across the men in the village.

"I don't think they're afraid of anything much," he said.

"You think this is where Garson has been bringing the girls?" Carol asked.

Fargo saw Annie's eyes on him. "No," he said. "These people would take their own girls if they had a mind to. They certainly wouldn't buy any from the likes of Max Garson."

"Well, they'd certainly know something about James Raynall," Carol said, and he shot her a curious glance.

"Why?" he asked.

"Because James Raynall would have made a point to get to know them. These are the kind of people that would fascinate his curious mind," Carol answered. "I'm sure they could tell us when he was here, perhaps even where he went."

Fargo's glance flicked to the darkening dusk and saw two small fires lighted in the village. He sent another slow survey across the village before he began to back away. "Let's get back to the horses. It'll be dark in minutes," he said.

"Back to the horses?" Carol frowned. "I want to visit these people and ask them about James."

"Back to the horses. We can talk there," Fargo said.

Carol didn't move. "We can talk here," she said.

Fargo's jaw grew tight. "The birdcalls and daylight forest noises have kept them from hearing us now. That'll end in a few minutes when it gets dark. They'll sure as hell hear us then. Now get back to the horses, dammit," he said, and started away in his crouching lope. He heard Annie follow and finally Carol bring up at the rear.

The night had descended when they reached the spot where they had left the horses, and he turned to face Carol as the first faint moonlight drifted down. "Talk," he growled.

"It's absolutely necessary that we visit with those people," she said.

"No," he snapped.

"I'm sure they can tell us about James," she said.

"They won't tell you shit about Raynall," Fargo said. "Even if he was there and managed to make friends with them, which I doubt."

"I don't. It'd be our first real lead," she insisted. "We must talk to them."

"It could be your last visit anywhere, honey," he said.

"I don't believe in exaggerated stories," she said stiffly.

"Neither do I," Fargo answered. "But I believe in what I know about people such as these. You go visiting and they'll eat you up."

"Nonsense," Carol said haughtily.

"We go on, come morning," Fargo said sternly. "I'm not going to poke into a cougar's den for something that might not even be there."

Carol's frown was made of protest. "You can't turn away from a chance for a real lead on James," she said.

"I can turn away from getting us all killed," Fargo said, and saw Carol look across at Annie.

"Of course, you agree with him," she sniffed with acid coating each word.

"You hired him for what he knows. I'd listen to him," Annie said.

"You wouldn't feel that way if you thought they knew where your cousin was," Carol snapped back.

"You're probably right, but I'd still listen to Fargo," Annie said. Carol spun away, strode to her horse and took her beef strips from her pack, marched to a distant tree, and sat down alone. "I hate women that sulk," Annie muttered to Fargo.

"Don't be bitchy," Fargo murmured. "She's used

to giving orders, not taking them." Annie sniffed disdainfully, went and got her own supper, and sat down close beside him as he began to eat. "We leave real quietly, come morning," he said. "Walk the horses till we're far enough away from here." Annie nodded and finished the sparse meal.

He saw that Carol stayed off by herself against the distant tree. Annie rose, took the short nightgown from her pack, and disappeared into the dark shadows for a moment. Fargo took the moment to undress and lay down on the soft bed of switchgrass.

Annie returned and lay down on her blanket a few dozen feet from him. Carol continued to stay by herself against the tree, but he saw she had wrapped the sheet around herself and laid down. She'd stop her sulking when morning came and she saw it wasn't having any effect, he was certain. He turned on his side and welcomed sleep.

The first tinge of morning had begun to filter down through the thick leaves when the faint sound woke him. He snapped his eyes open and saw Carol beside him on one knee. She had already dressed, he noted as he pushed up on one elbow, and she put a finger to her lips. "Apologies," she whispered. "In advance. You'll see that I was right." He frowned up at her, the vestiges of sleep still clinging to him, when she brought her arm around in a quick, short arc. He glimpsed the butt of the pistol in her hand but too late to do more than half-turn before the gun crashed down onto his head. The moment of sharp pain shot through him and he was dimly aware of his head falling backward before the silent void of unconsciousness enveloped him.

He lay in nothingness until finally he felt something, sensation, the first glimmer of consciousness returning. Coldness, first, then wetness, and his mind struggled into waking. He blinked as he felt the wetness again, water against his face, and he pulled his eyes open. Annie's pert face came into view, concern in it turning to relief as he pushed up on one elbow. Still clothed in the short, high-necked nightshirt, she pressed a damp rag onto a spot atop his head, just back of his hairline, and he winced.

"What happened? Where's Carol?" she asked.

"Gone. She slugged me and took off," Fargo muttered.

"To the forest people," Annie said.

"Of course, goddamn headstrong little fool," Fargo bit out, and pushed to his feet. He ignored the stab of pain in his head and began to pull on clothes.

"I woke, saw you just lying there, and knew something was wrong. When I went over to you, I saw the blood trickling down your forehead," Annie said.

His hand curled around her shoulder for a moment. "Thanks," he said, and she returned a quick, almost shy smile and hurried into the trees as he continued dressing. He was strapping on his gun belt when she returned. Carol had sense enough to leave her horse, he noted as he spied the brown mare near the Ovaro. He dropped into his crouching lope and started toward the lake, Annie but a few paces behind. He slowed when he neared the water and saw two long alligators sunning themselves on the shore. He changed directions to move closer to the curve of the shoreline where the village spread out. When he pushed through the last of the trees, the village was but a few dozen yards away. He dropped to one knee and found Annie close beside him. "She's there," he murmured before he saw her as he heard the excited murmuring of voices and saw the figures crowded into a long half-circle.

Three women and a handful of youngsters moved to the end of the half-circle and let him see into the center of the knot of villagers. Carol faced a half-dozen men. One, tall and lean, with a short very black beard and burning black eyes, walked slowly around her.

"He must be the head of the clan," Annie whispered. Fargo nodded and watched the man halt in front of Carol. She was holding her cool composure, Fargo noted, not without admiration.

"Tell us again how you come by here, girl," the man said, his voice carrying clearly to where Fargo crouched with Annie.

"I told you, I'm looking for James Raynall. I thought he might have stayed with you," Carol said calmly.

"That's why, not how," the man said, his voice growing sharp. "How'd you come here finding us?"

"James Raynall told me he was coming this way. I've been following along south. I just came onto you by accident," Carol said.

"Just walking, all by your little self," the man said, suspicion harsh in his voice now.

"That's right," Carol said carefully.

"She's damn lying to us, Lucius," one of the other men interrupted.

"I do believe she is," the one called Lucius said with a touch of sadness. His movement was lightning-quick, a backhanded blow to Carol's face that made her head spin and sent her sprawling on the ground with a cry of pain. The tall, lanky figure bent over her as she lay on one elbow and glared up at him. "Now, you didn't just come walking through the Ocala all by yourself, girl. Who you be with?" he asked.

"Nobody," Carol said, and he yanked her to her feet. "I just want to know if James Raynall was here. I didn't come to bother you."

The man smiled and revealed long, pointy teeth. "You're lyin', girl. But that's no real matter. You're not going to tell anything or go anywhere. You be one of us now," he said.

"I'm not one of you and I demand that you let me go," Carol said, still commanding a cool loftiness.

The man snapped his fingers and two of the others stepped forward and took hold of Carol's arms. "Take her inside for now. Tie her up good. She's a special one, she is," Lucius said. "Meanwhile, the rest of you go find whoever she be with. They not be far, I'm thinking."

Fargo waited a moment to watch as Carol was led into one of the more substantial huts. Then he rose and moved backward, Annie beside him. He hurried to where they had left the horses, took the brown mare's reins along with those of the pinto, and walked the horses from the spot. He pushed deep into the forest, Annie at his heels, and halted only after he'd gone a half-mile or so into the very densest part of the already heavily foliaged terrain. "This ought to be far enough," he said. "They won't search the whole forest. They'll spread out around the lake and maybe a hundred yards or so in from the shore. They'll be slow and thorough, but when they don't find anything they'll go back."

Annie tossed him a sidelong glance. "Then we go on?" she slid at him.

"No," he said, and saw her lips edge a faint smile.

"Figured that's what you'd say," she murmured.

"Would you really want me to say anything else?" he asked.

She screwed up her pert face for a moment. "No. Yet a person makes their bed they have to lie in it," Annie said. "I want to go after Una, not end up dead because Carol decided to be a damn fool."

"Seems as though you don't know which is right," Fargo said.

"I guess not," Annie glowered.

"Sometimes you save damn fools in spite of themselves," Fargo said.

She fastened a narrowed glance at him and a little sound came from her lips. "Yes, dammit, so you do," she muttered. "You made your point."

He slid to the ground. "We wait here till afternoon. I want to give them plenty of time to get back to the village and settle down." She lowered herself beside him, a tiny glower on her face. He put a hand on her shoulder, his voice not ungentle. "You can sit this one out," he said. "I'll understand."

"No, I'm with you, whatever happens," she said. "You have any ideas on how we can get her out?"

"Not a one," Fargo said honestly.

"Damn, you're something special," Annie said.

"Something will come to me after I take another look at the village," he said.

She shook her head in a kind of awe and her brown eyes stayed on him. "You're something special in a lot of ways," she said. "You saved my neck in town, then when Garson tried to burn down my place. Most men would've come looking for thanks. You haven't even looked differently at me."

He laughed. "Maybe you just didn't notice," he said.

He watched her turn his words in her mind, her pert face entirely serious. "In that case, it's time for noticing," she said and he felt the surprise clutch at him as she began to unbutton her shirt. She wriggled her shoulders and the shirt fell from her and he found himself taking in very round, high breasts, perfectly shaped, both tanned with small pink nipples, cradled by a small pink circle. Round shoulders and a slightly barrel-chested rib cage completed a firm, compact torso. She rose to her knees, turned her hips, yanked off her riding britches and bloomers with one quick motion, and turned to him. He saw a slightly convex little belly, full hips, sturdy, compact thighs that were nonetheless trim and nicely formed, and a small, neat little dark triangle.

Annie very definitely had her own beauty, and part of it was that she radiated a simmering sensual energy, not unlike a seedpod straining to burst forth. He opened buttons, threw off his gun belt, and felt himself already straining at the sight of her quietly anxious waiting. As he shed the last garment, Annie's eyes on him widened and he heard her faint gasp. "Oh, Jeez," she breathed and almost flew at him, arms coming around his neck, high, firm breasts warm as they pressed into his chest. He swung her onto her back, his mouth coming down upon hers as one thought exploded in his mind. Carol had been right. Totally, absolutely right. Then Annie's lips on his erased all further thoughts and the flesh took command.

His hand cupped around one firm breast, caressed, and stroked its high, round contours, and Annie made a small gurgling sound. Her hands moved up and down his back in a frantic exploration, stroking, digging in, becoming small fists that pounded against him. His mouth found her breasts, drew in one, then the other, sucked hard, and she cried out in pure joy. "Jeez, jeez, yes, oh, God, more, more . . ." Annie's convex little belly pushed up against his rigidness, heat against heat, rubbed, pressed, and her firm, young thighs fell open and clasped around him, then fell open again. Little crying sounds came from her, half-choking sobs of pure ecstasy, and he felt himself swept up by the explosion of frenzied wanting that was hers.

She slid her body up and down against him, half-screamed as his organ came near her dark warmth, pressed again, and screamed again. "Jeez, oh, oh, aaaaaiiiii . . ." Annie cried out and he felt her pushing hard against him, sliding down, then upward. He drew back, found her wetness, and entered, slowly, but she would have none of that. She thrust forward and her scream was muffled against his chest, but she thrust again and again, and he found himself unable to find gentleness as her frenzy swept him along.

"Jeez, yes, yes, yes . . . ah, yes, oh, my God, oh, yes . . . oh, oh," Annie flung out, words connected by moaning sobs of eagerness. He felt her firm thighs tight around his waist, sweet and wonderful bonds of pleasure. She pulled his mouth down to her breasts. She was tight around him, outer and inner tightness, and pushing and pumping without ceasing until suddenly her thighs fell from around him and he felt her sturdy legs straighten out. She rose under him, arched her compact, strong body, and carried him upward with her. She seemed suddenly frozen in space and her cries had turned to short, gasped breaths.

With an exploding suddenness, her scream tore from someplace deep inside her, a shout and a cry, ecstasy bursting all confinement. "Y-e-s-ssssssss, yes, yes, ye-sssssssssss," Annie cried out, and quivered against him. He felt himself erupt within her. The moment hung in eternity even as it vanished in the blink of an eye and her moan became a soft, cooing sound as she fell back, arms, legs, hands, everything wrapped around him, the senses refusing to recede, flesh clinging to pleasure.

He lay with her until she finally went limp. He finally drew from her warm wetness, to lay beside her, on one elbow, his eyes enjoying the still-tingling, compact beauty of her, the high, round breasts still quivering and her entire body damp with tiny beads of perspiration. She smelled wonderfully female, the faintly dusky odor exciting of itself. She had made love, he found himself realizing, with the same pugnacious, driving force with which she did everything. Her own kind of beauty, he pondered as he enjoyed her compact, firm body. Her own kind of heat, sensuality wrapped in aggressive energy.

She smiled, picking up his appraisal. "Surprised?" she asked.

"That's the right word," he said.

"I got to thinking that if we don't come out of this, if it goes wrong, I'd never have another chance," she said. "And I'd probably never find anyone like you again."

"Just all of a sudden like that?" he asked, and she allowed a sheepish little smile.

"No, I'd been thinking about it every night," she said. "But this pushed it from thinking to doing."

He pulled her to him. "I'm glad," he said, and kissed her breasts. Annie let out a groan, enjoying his mouth on her. Then she pulled back and he saw the dark fire in her eyes, her compact body somehow again sending out little waves of electricity. He reached out, pressed his hand over the small, neat triangle, and felt the soft rise of her pubic mound. He pressed harder, his hand cupping around the base of the triangle, and Annie let out a high-pitched squeal of delight. She swung her legs out so she could press upward against his palm.

"Yes, damn, yes, yes, yes," she murmured, and he saw the dark wildness come into her eyes. He touched, caressed the moist, secluded lips. Annie's hips turned, twisted, thrust upward, and her hands grabbed for him at once. He tried to slow her wanting, hold back her frenzied desire, but again, she would have none of that. Her hands found his pulsating warmth, held tightly, and cried out in discovered pleasure. "Oh. Jeez, jeez, oh God, I want . . . I want . . ." she gasped, and pulled him to her, pushed her hips upward for him, and once again she was pushing, thrusting, pumping, completely immersing every part of herself in the pleasures of the senses.

Her round, high breasts were damp as he drew first one and then the other into his mouth, and Annie's gasping cries had become a staccato obbligato to her fierce embrace of passion. It was all new to her. She had no desire to hold back or prolong. Perhaps she never would, he realized, but certainly not now. He went with her, matching her headlong rush of wanting. Now Annie Dowd was all raging excitement, the seed-pod bursting in all directions, each new sensation a delicious discovery. He felt the sudden pull of her legs and arms clasped around him and let her roll him onto his back where, with a little squeal of delight, she pushed herself down on him.

She half-rose, came down, half-rose again, came down harder, thrust herself again and again, as deeply and wholly as she could while she flung her head back and let out cries of pleasure. His hands curled around her round, high breasts as they bounced, and suddenly he felt her rise, hold for a fraction of a second in midair as her mouth opened soundlessly and he saw the wildness sweep through her eyes. "Oh, my God, now, now . . . iiiiiieeeee," Annie screamed as she came down onto him, held there tight against him, and quivered as she clung to him with thighs, arms, hands, every part of her compact body tightened against him. He let himself come with her as she continued to violently quiver as tiny little gasped sounds came from her hips.

Then, finally, the moment exploded away and Annie let out a half-cry of almost despair. She fell forward over him, deep, harsh breaths coming from her until, with a shuddered sigh, she fell onto her side against him. She turned at once, wrapped her arms around him, and childlike, she was asleep in seconds. He smiled as he lay with her. She had been a surprise in more ways than one, and now there was an added reason to rescue Carol, he mused. Carol had certainly been on target about Annie. Now he wanted to find out if Annie was as right about her. He continued to wear the tiny smile of anticipation as he closed his eyes on the thought and let himself nap in the heat of the afternoon sun.

6

Fargo woke when he reacted to the sun as it moved westward, its burning heat no longer as intense. He moved, sat up, and Annie opened her eyes and instantly reached for him again. He eluded her arms and she blinked. "Get dressed. Time to go calling," he said. She rose to her feet with a hint of a pout, her compact body—hips thrust out, high firm breasts—all still radiating her aggressive sensuality. He turned away or knew he'd find himself reaching for her.

He dressed and Annie had clothes on as he finished and walked to the horses. "We'll ride back until we near the lake," he said, swung onto the Ovaro, and took the brown mare's reins in hand.

He rode slowly through the dense foliage, back to where he had first left the horses and dismounted. "Look around," he said to Annie. "You may have to find your way back here alone in the dark. Pick out markers."

She glanced left, then right, circled the area with her eyes, and halted at a spot a dozen feet away. "There, that tupelo with a cotton gum on each side of it," she said. "And that laurel oak with the twisted lower branches."

"Good enough," he grunted, and moved on foot toward the lake as the forest began to take on the dimness of twilight. He reached the shore, Annie beside him, and halted as a huge gator climbed from the lake, switched its powerful tail, and flattened a pair of small shrubs. The gator moved slowly, made clicking noises with its jaws, and then slid back into the lake. Fargo saw two more knobby-headed shapes move slowly through the water. "Damn lake's full of them," he grunted as he crept forward toward the village. He stayed crouched in the trees, then moved closer to the curve of the lake where the village spread in careless profusion.

Women were tending open-pit cooking fires. Some young girls, bare-breasted and shoeless, carried water buckets. Some of the men dragged nets of fish from the shore and others simply lounged against the huts. Fargo's eyes traveled slowly across the village and found the tall man with the short black beard. Lucius was seated on a stump, a stafflike gnarled cane in one hand as he surveyed the village with patriarchal approval. He moved his gaze on to the other end of the sprawling line of huts and then brought his eyes back to the house where they had taken Carol.

"She's still in there," Fargo said. "I hope," he added grimly.

The Trailsman surveyed the village again with a slow, careful scan as thoughts formed themselves in his mind. The forest people felt completely safe. They'd have no sentries posted. That was a plus. But to reach the house where they'd put Carol, he'd have to pick his way through most of the village. They were all light-sleepers, he wagered grimly, forever tuned to any unusual sound in their forest bastion. It was part of people such as these, as much a part of the forest as any of its wild creatures. He could make his way alone, he'd no fears about that. He knew how to step as quietly as a panther, how to place a foot without cracking a twig, when and how to move without breathing, and how to listen as he moved, always listen. But picking his way back with Carol would be another matter. He grimaced at the thought. It would be all but impossible, he realized. She had no training in the ways of silence and stealth, and perhaps would be in no condition for it.

He swore silently and scanned the village again as the dusk deepened. Suddenly his eyes halted at the collection of off-shaped boats that were pulled up on the shore. He glanced at Annie and saw she had followed his eyes and now turned a frown at him. "I told you something would come to me," he said.

"Get her out by boat?"

"Bull's-eye," he said. "I'll make my way in alone and bring her out and take one of the boats."

"What if something goes wrong and they see you?"

"I'll row across to the other side of the lake and circle back on foot."

"I just sit here and wait?" Annie asked.

"Not exactly. I'll fill it in for you later," Fargo said as he saw Lucius rise to his feet and take the few steps to the main house.

"Have them bring her out," Lucius said to one of the young girls, who hurried into the house.

Darkness was moving in quickly now, and as Fargo watched, three of the men lighted a half-dozen torches that were pushed into the soft earth. In moments, the village was well-illuminated and he saw others move toward the house to form a semicircle. The figures emerged through the door, Carol, wrists bound separately, each held by a woman. They pulled her to a halt in front of Lucius, who held his gnarled cane with prophetlike demeanor. "We could not find your friends," Lucius said. "I would wager they have gone off and left you. It would be the wise thing to do."

"Amen," Annie whispered, and Fargo shot her a disapproving glance.

"I told you, I was alone," Carol said, and Fargo

93

saw that she continued to cling to her cool, disdainful composure.

"Stop lying," Lucius said sharply. "Not that it matters now. But lying is a sin."

"So is holding people against their will," Carol snapped. "Especially those who don't mean you any harm."

"You came prying. You are ours now, just as if you be a fish we caught coming near shore," Lucius said. He put aside his gnarled stick and slowly walked around Carol. "She is indeed a handsome wench," he said to the others as he completed his circle. "The question is, who shall have her first?"

"You bastard," Fargo heard Carol fling back. "You bunch of stupid, illiterate morons."

Lucius' slap spun her head around and only the two women holding on to the ropes at her wrists stopped her from falling. Lucius stepped forward, seized Carol by her dusty-blond hair, and yanked her onto her knees. "I want to think about what will best suit you, filthy-mouthed bitch. I think one of our young boys ready to become a man should maybe have you first. Then the rest of us will have our turn and then the women that want to," he said. "But I will think the night on it."

"Bastard," Carol spit out, but some of her composure had left her, Fargo noted as Lucius pulled her to her feet. With one hand, he ripped the front of her shirt open as he stepped back and Fargo glimpsed her full breasts. Lucius motioned to four more of the women to step forward.

"Take her inside and teach her the meaning of obedience," he said. "But I want no heavy marks, no bruises. She is too beautiful for that. I want her nakedness unmarked for our young men. Use your switches and then see she is tied well."

The women nodded and Fargo watched them take

up long switches fashioned of stems bound together as they followed the two women who pulled Carol inside the hut. Fargo heard Annie's whisper at his side. "The son of a bitch. I could put a bullet between his eyes," she said.

"And we'd never get Carol out," Fargo said.

She swore again and fell silent.

It took only a few moments for Carol's first cry of pain to spiral from the hut. Another followed, then another, in between curses she flung back, but soon she only yelped with each blow. Finally she stopped and the four women emerged, hair disheveled and wiping perspiration from their faces. But they wore sadistic smiles, Fargo saw. There was little difference between the men and the women of these inbred, primitive people, he decided.

A full moon had come up. In the open expanse of the lake and the cleared area around the village, it brought a soft light that took over as the torches were put out. The figures began to drift to their huts as Fargo watched, though a fair number curled up on the ground outside.

"How long do we wait?" Annie asked.

"I'll give them another hour to make sure they're all asleep, maybe a little more," Fargo said. "Then I'll go back and bring the horses. You'll wait here with the horses. If everything goes right, I'll row back here with Carol. If it doesn't, I'll have her swim for shore. You meet her with the horses and take off south."

"What about you?"

"I'll catch up to you," Fargo said.

Annie's eyes went to the lake and he saw the knobby protuberances floating silently a dozen yards from the shore, only a moment's flash of yellow eyes giving evidence that they weren't logs. "She's not going to make it swimming for shore," Annie said.

"I'll try to see that she does," Fargo said. "If it comes to that."

Annie cast a sidelong glance at him. "You stay here. I'll go get the horses," she said.

He agreed with a nod. "Walk them back, real slow," he said, and she hurried away to disappear into the dense foliage.

Fargo returned his eyes to the village and saw Lucius step from one of the smaller huts, walk to the shoreline, and slowly scan the night shadows. The man stayed, kept looking, and Fargo swore under his breath. Lucius sensed something. Intuition, sixth sense, an inner warning system beyond defining by logic and beyond explaining in rational terms. But it was there, in the way the sheep know the wolf is near before they can see, hear, or smell him. In the way a horse knows a cougar is on the prowl, and the chickens feel the presence of the fox.

It was there, made of the undefinable yet so very real in its own way. Lucius was feeling it. But he was human, a backward, primitive human, yet still a human, and unable to ignore the human reliance on reason and the material senses. He heard nothing, saw nothing, and smelled nothing in the night, and he finally turned and went back into the hut. The human thing to do, Fargo smiled. But he would sleep uneasily, Fargo knew unable to completely dismiss the vestigial, inner senses.

Fargo sat back and watched two women emerge from one of the huts. They whisked off dresses as they placed reed mats on the ground and curled up naked in the hot and steamy night. His eyes went to the lake, where he watched the protruding knobs that were a gator's eyes move past him in absolute silence. Fargo turned as he heard the soft rustle of leaves behind him and he saw Annie leading the horses. He motioned for her to leave the horses a dozen feet back, and she came forward with the big Sharps in her hand.

"Just in case," she said. "If I have to shoot from here, I want something that'll make a bigger hole more on target than a six-gun."

"That'll do it," Fargo agreed. "Now remember, if it goes wrong, I'll try to get Carol to shore. They don't have any horses so you two can get away fast and clean."

"Get her in by boat or she'll never make it," Annie said.

"Don't be so damn gloomy. I've heard of people swimming past gators," he said.

Annie shook her head adamantly. "Not swimming. Floating. Just floating, not making any move that'll get the gator's attention. And only a few of those have made it. If she's trying to get away, she'll have to be swimming."

Fargo let Annie's words sink in. "I'll remember that," he said, and turned his gaze toward the silent village of huts. "Time to go," he said, and before he could rise, Annie's arms were around him, one hand still holding the rifle, her lips on his. Finally she pulled back.

"Good luck," she murmured. "Don't get yourself killed to save her dumb ass. She brought it on herself."

"You having memory problems again?" He smiled and she looked away.

"Damn you," she murmured. "Go."

Fargo rose into a crouch and set off around the curve of the shore, keeping to the very edge of the trees. He was at the edge of the village in minutes and sank to one knee, his eyes peering past the huts. Moving on silent steps, he began to enter the sprawling collection of dwellings. He reached the first one, started past when he sank to one knee, the Colt in his hand as he heard the sounds from inside the hut. He listened and a grim smile touched his lips. The sounds were unmistakable, soft groanings of pleasure, gasped exchanges. No male voice, only the interwoven groans of young women.

He moved on and wondered how much more of the village was still not asleep. But the next huts he passed were silent, and it wasn't till he had reached the center of the village that he heard murmured voices from one of the other huts, a man's voice first, then a woman's. He went on quickly and skirted the two naked women sleeping on the reed mats, both bony, gaunt bodies. He stepped softly, passed the two women, and reached the largest of the huts where they had taken Carol. The door was half-open and he caught a faint flicker of light from inside the room. He carefully slipped his big frame through the opened part of the doorway, taking care not to move the door. It no doubt creaked.

An almost burned-out candle in a corner of the room provided the dim, flickering light, and he saw three of the village women lying on mats in different parts of the large, single room. He found Carol in one corner, her clothes on and her wrists bound together, her arms stretched upward where a rope bound her to a wall peg. His eyes went to her ankles and saw they were tied also. One of the women slept only a scant six feet from where Carol lay, breathing heavily in sleep. Fargo crept forward on the dirt floor of the hut and reached Carol. He pressed one hand over her mouth and her eyes snapped open at once, wide with fear.

She blinked, and the fear turned to overwhelming relief as she recognized him. He drew his hand from her mouth and reached down to the calf holster around his leg and drew out the double-edged throwing knife. He severed Carol's wrist bonds first and her arms dropped to her sides as her head came against his chest. He pushed her back gently, one finger to his lips, and severed the ropes around her ankles. He had just put the knife back into its holster when he heard the sound at his right; he spun around to see the woman nearest him sitting up, surprise on her face as she stared at him.

He moved with the speed of silent lightning, one quick step just as the woman's mouth opened to scream. His blow, a short, downward arc, clipped her on her jaw and she toppled backward on the mat, unconscious. But she landed with a thud and Fargo spun to glance at the other two women. He saw them both wake, sit up, and peer across at him. One rolled onto her side, came up, and reached into her dress. Fargo saw the last of the flickering candle glint on the skinning knife in her hand. He reached down, yanked Carol to her feet. "Start running, honey," he hissed as he headed for the door. The woman darted forward to cut him off, the knife upraised as the other one let out a piercing shriek of alarm.

Fargo charged for the door, Carol at his heels, and the woman, wild-haired and lean, half-crouched and swung the knife as he reached her. But he twisted away, expecting the blow, sank a short, hard left into her ribs, which sent her sprawling to one side. He saw her manage to avoid falling, recover her footing, and spin again with the knife. But he was racing from the hut with Carol as the woman joined the other one in screaming the alarm. Fargo ran for the line of rowboats pulled up on the shore as he heard the village come awake. He motioned to a flat-prowed stubby craft and Carol climbed in as he turned to see a half-dozen men run from the huts, some still pulling on trousers. One was Lucius, and he saw the man reach for a long-barreled rifle standing against the side of a hut.

Fargo dug heels deep into the soft shore mud as he pushed the boat into the water and dived headlong into it as a shot hurtled over his head. He took hold of one of the two short oars on the floor of the boat, stayed low as he reached over the side, and began to paddle. The village was fully awake now, shouts and curses intermingling with gunshots that whistled past the boat. He wasn't getting any thrust paddling from the floorboards and he rose to the one piece of wood that constituted a seat and put his shoulders fully into paddling. The boat picked up speed, though its flat prow hardly let it move quickly. Carol, on the floor of the boat, suddenly called out. "They're coming after us," she said, and he looked back to see Lucius and some of the other men pushing off in three boats.

He slowly turned the stubby craft and started for the shore, where Annie waited, but a volley of shots made him drop low inside the boat. He glimpsed a sudden flurry of armorlike shapes in the water as he rose again and resumed paddling until another volley of shots made him drop low again. He raised his head to peer over the edge of the boat and saw one of the other boats, a faster craft with a real prow, moving sideways to cut him off while the other two drew closer to him. Suddenly the sharp, crisp bark of rifle fire erupted, a sound he instantly recognized, and then he heard the shouts of sudden terror.

He peered over the edge of the boat again and saw all three of the pursuing craft beginning to sink. "Goddamn," he bit out with a laugh. Annie had blown holes into each of the boats. The boat with Lucius and two other men was the largest and sturdiest of all, and he saw Lucius ordering the men to row for shore. Fargo's eyes went to the other two boats. They were almost underwater and he saw the two men in each craft throw themselves into the water and strike out for the village. But he also saw the half-dozen shapes materialize out of the depths of the lake as if by magic to converge on the swimming figures.

The first scream of terror and pain split the night, and he saw one of the swimmers throw his arms up and then disappear under the surface.

"Oh, God," Carol gasped as another figure screamed and Fargo saw the man being whirled in the water as tremendous jaws clasped him around his waist. The gator continued to turn his victim in the water, whirling his own huge form at the same time, powerful tail slapping hard and sending up sprays of water. Somehow, the man continued to scream until the alligator pulled him underwater.

More gators converged on the two men still swimming and Fargo threw a glance at Lucius. The larger boat was sinking now, but it was close to shore. They'd just make it, Fargo saw as he paddled furiously toward the shoreline, where Annie waited. He had gone perhaps another six yards when a huge shape emerged from the water at the side of the boat, tremendous jaws open and a violent hissing sound coming from the huge mouth. The jaws came down on the side of the boat, snapping the paddle in two and crushing the light wood of the boat as though it were paper. The water rushed into the boat even as the big gator still had his jaws clamped around the wood.

Carol screamed and Fargo shot a harsh glance at her. "Shut up," he yelled, and she fell silent. The gator was letting go of the boat, but he'd come in for another attack, Fargo knew. "Can you swim underwater?" he asked Carol, and she nodded. "Start swimming, honey. Stay underwater as long as you can, surface for air and go down again. No splashing and thrashing around."

She nodded and swung herself over the other side of the boat just as the gator appeared again, huge jaws open and hissing. Fargo watched Carol disappear under the surface, gathered himself, and dived past the open jaws and into the water. The alligator turned instantly with one whip of his huge tail, but Fargo was moving at him from the side. As the huge amphibian's jaws snapped open and shut as he cast around for his prey, Fargo flung himself onto the gator's back. His arms wrapped tight around the beast's neck, he clung with all his strength as the alligator instantly spun in the water, using his tail to turn over and over as he tried to dislodge the object on its back.

Fargo used every muscle in his body to cling to the alligator, and as he surfaced during one spin, he glimpsed at least three other gators swimming in circles around the thrashing water. He drew in a deep breath and held it as the gator dived a few feet and shot to the surface again. But as the huge amphibian started to spin again, Fargo felt his muscles weakening. He knew he'd never be able to hold on for another fury of spinning and he didn't want to be thrown a dozen feet away, perhaps to land beside one of the other alligators. He released his grip and dived straight down, yanked at his calf, and drew the double-edged throwing knife.

The gator was directly above him and had stopped spinning at once. But he'd be diving down, seeking whatever had clung to him. Fargo kicked upward with all his strength, the knife outstretched as he held the blade with both hands. He drove it into the softest spot in the armored creature's body, the underside of the neck just below the jaws. He drove the blade in to the hilt and brought it downward, the one razor-sharp edge slicing a deep cut partway to the gator's belly. Yanking the blade free, he kicked out and swam away as the dark-red liquid instantly gushed into the water.

His lungs burning and about to burst, he managed to swim another few feet before he surfaced and gulped in deep drafts of air. Taking a moment to regain his breath, he saw the four gnarled shapes converging on the bloodied gator. He drew a deep breath, went under the surface, and struck out for the shore. When he came up for air, he glanced back at a scene of furiously thrashing tails and sheets of water sent flying into the air. If Carol had made it to the shore, she and Annie would be gone now, racing through the night. He had just reached the shoreline when he saw the dark figures running through the trees.

Fargo sank back and moved sideways to the buttressed bark of a big cypress. Lucius had seen the furious thrashing of the gator, but he wanted to make sure no one had managed to get away. He'd taken his men and run from the village, around the curve to where the rifle fire had erupted, and now they were combing the area. Fargo stayed beside the giant, buttressed roots, squeezed in between one of the tree's knees, and watched the search wind to a halt. They had found nothing, which meant that Annie, at least, had gotten away. Had Carol been with her? he wondered. And it meant one thing more.

Annie would have waited for him and seen Lucius and the others coming. She'd have stayed as long as she dared before fleeing and she had taken the Ovaro with her rather than leave the horse to be found. Fargo allowed a wry smile to edge his lips. Annie was too much an admirer of fine horses to leave the Ovaro to the likes of the forest people. He watched Lucius and his followers move around the slow curve on their way back to the village, and he left the cypress and drifted to shore. He pulled himself onto the bank and moved back into the thick tree cover, where he sank down and pulled off his wet clothes. He sank down on a soft bed of nut moss after spreading his clothes out. There were only a few hours of night left, but the hot, steamy air would dry his things out enough for an hour of morning sun to finish.

He slept quickly, his body feeling the effects of the battle with the gator. When morning came, he took another hour to let the filtered sunlight thoroughly dry his clothes. He rose then, dressed, and ate some fruit he found nearby. He made his way to the spot Annie had waited with the horses. She would have fled inland and south, he knew, and he began to move through the trees. Hoofprints were still visible in the softer ground near the lake, and he spied the narrow passageway he was certain Annie had taken. Hoofprints still visible, still only hours old, confirmed his certainty, and he followed in their path. When they vanished where the grass had time to spring back, bruised and broken young branches on both sides of the narrow passage marked the trail.

The passage widened a little, but the overhead, thick branches of the larger cotton gums and satinleafs grew lower. He had set a steady, long-striding pace with its own swinging rhythm that let him cover ground almost tirelessly. It was becoming clear that Annie had kept riding through the night when he drew to a halt, his ears picking up the sound from ahead of him. He listened and it came again, a horse blowing air through its nostrils. Dropping to a loping crouch, he moved forward, cautiously pushing his way through a dense clump of trees that all but blocked the path. He saw the horse, the brown mare, first, then his Ovaro.

He darted forward and saw Carol spin, the six-gun in her hand, which she lowered as she saw him. His eyes went past her to Annie lying on the blanket, her eyes closed, the short-legged light bay in the background. She had a damp towel across her forehead. "God, I've been hoping you'd find us," Carol said.

"It's been a long walk. What happened?" Fargo

questioned as he stepped to Annie's side. She didn't move.

"We were riding hard last night. I told her we were going too fast. It got so dark in that passage we could hardly see. She smashed her head into a low branch and fell. I carried her here," Carol said. "She hasn't moved since."

Fargo bent down, ran his hand across Annie's face, then down to her breastbone. "She's burning up," he said.

"I know. I've been putting cold towels on her for hours. There's a little stream a few yards into the trees," Carol said.

"She's in some kind of coma." Fargo frowned. "The body has reacted by a high fever. There's nothing to do now but try and get the fever down."

"That's a fresh towel I just put on her," Carol said, and Fargo rose and stepped to the Ovaro and began to unsaddle the horse.

"I expect we'll be here a spell," he said. When he set the saddle down, he lowered himself against a tree trunk and Carol came over and sat down beside him.

"I thought that gator had you," she said. "When I reached shore, Annie told me you'd purposely pulled his attention to you so I could make it."

"Couldn't think of any other way you'd make it," he said, and her muted blue eyes were dark with a mixture of pain and gratitude.

"I didn't deserve that. It was all my fault, my stupid stubbornness," she said.

His eyes remained ice-floe cold. "That's sure enough right," he said. "The women gave you an old-fashioned hiding in the hut." She nodded and met his hard stare. "That's the only reason I'm not doing it now," he growled, and she looked away.

She rose, took another towel from a small stack next to Annie, and went into the trees. He heard her at the stream and watched as she returned with the towel wet and cool and replaced the one on Annie's forehead with it. She sat down beside the unmoving form, drew her knees up, and rested her head against them, a silent, penitent figure. No act for his benefit, he decided, watching her as she replaced fresh towels every half-hour. She was genuinely conscience-stricken and she stepped back silently each time he went to Annie to check on her.

"She's still too damn hot," Fargo grunted, and swore inside himself at the feeling of utter helplessness that embraced him. The only hopeful signs were that her breathing was steady and that the lump atop her head had gone down considerably. He rose and paused beside Carol. "I'm going to get some sleep so's I can spell you during the night," he said.

"I can handle it," she said, a touch of defensiveness in her voice.

"I'll spell you," he said, and she retreated into silence. He picked out a shade place under one of the gums and slept into the early night. He woke to see the moonlight outlining Carol sitting beside Annie and he rose and walked to her. "Did you eat?" he asked.

"Some things from my saddlebag. I'm not very hungry," she said.

"Any changes?" Fargo asked, and Carol's grim glance was his answer. "I'll take over now. Get yourself some sleep," he said.

Carol showed fatigue in the way her willowy body rose and gathered her things. She reappeared in the nightgown, wrapped in the sheet, and lay down a dozen yards away.

Fargo took one of the towels, found the small stream among the trees, and replaced the cold compress on Annie's forehead. He lay down beside her, napped in spurts throughout the night, and continued to apply the cold compresses.

When morning came and Carol disappeared into the trees to dress, Fargo changed the compress once again and grasped for small victories. Annie was still unchanged, but she had gotten no worse, the fever no higher. It was a backhanded kind of comfort, but he embraced it nonetheless.

He let Carol sit with her and begin the patient task of trying to keep the fever in check with fresh compresses every half-hour to an hour. He curled up in the shade of the big cotton gum, and when the day moved into afternoon, he rose and took the rifle from its saddlecase. "I've had enough of dried beef jerky," he said to Carol as he passed her and moved into the trees.

The marsh was not far away. He had smelled its damp odor and soon saw the long, uneven-leafed swamp lilies. He also saw the dark-brown furred forms he had noted at every marsh they had passed along the way, the same general size as the cottontail but more gray-brown in color. He dropped to one knee, put the rifle to his shoulder, and watched the marsh rabbits hop their way through the thin cattails. His first shot brought down one more than large enough for a dinner for three. He retrieved it, watched an eastern diamondback slither away, wanting no more to do with him than he did with it.

He returned to where Carol sat beside Annie, used the throwing knife to carve a section of branch into a spit, and then skinned the rabbit. With a small but hot fire, he began to roast dinner. He had spotted a small growth of wild onion and chopped two small bulbs to sprinkle over the rabbit. The meal was ready soon after darkness fell and he heard Carol call to him.

"Fargo, come here," she said, excitement in her voice, and he hurried to her. "She's cooled some,"

Carol said, and he dropped to one knee and ran his hands over Annie's head and neck.

"She has," he agreed. "Let's keep up what we've been doing. Meanwhile, dinner's ready."

Carol rose and went back with him to the spit, where he removed the rabbit and used his knife to cut off the savory meat. Carol ate hungrily beside him, and when they were finished, he cut off the meat that was still left and wrapped it in leaves. He doused the fire's remains and the moon came out and he took another look at Annie. She was definitely cooler and he decided to apply the cold compresses every hour. As the night deepened, he moved to the edge of the little cleared area and rested his back against a tupelo. Carol took her things into the trees to change, but when she emerged, she carried no sheet wrapped around her. She wore only the silk nightgown as she came toward him and sank to the ground at his side.

Her breasts were lovely as they pressed against the thin, silken garment. She leaned forward, her blue eyes searching his face, her arms lifting, sliding around his neck. "I have to," she murmured. "I have to." Her lips, full softness, touched his, pressed, pushed his mouth open, and he felt her tongue dart forward, smoothly exciting, then pull back, and she drew away for a moment.

"You have to?" he asked, and she nodded, her patrician face grave. "Feeling guilty? Trying to make it up to me?" he asked.

"No, nothing as cleansing as that," Carol said.

"What, then?" he prodded.

"Seizing the moment. Taking hold of a chance that might never come again. I've wanted you from the first day we met. It exploded inside me right then. That's why I was so angry when you brought Annie along," she said. "It hasn't happened to me since I was very young. There was a farm boy, worked for my dad. He made me explode inside the same way. And now you. No better reason. No other excuses."

"That'll do," he said, reached out both hands, and slipped the straps of the nightgown from her shoulders. It fell to her waist. He took in full breasts, beautifully curved at the bottoms, a deep-pink nipple protruding firmly on each, centered against a lighter pink areola. A long, narrow rib cage, tapering down to a narrow waist, fitted the long line of her breasts with symmetrical simplicity. She rose and the rest of the nightgown fell to the grass, and he saw narrow hips, not an ounce of excess flesh to them, a flat abdomen and equally flat belly, and below, a triangle of dusty blond that matched her hair. Long, lean, and lovely legs were sensuous willow wands. He reached out one arm and she stepped forward. He thrust his arm between her thighs and Carol cried out as he lifted and swung her in a half-circle to the ground.

His hand stayed cupped between her thighs as he brought his lips to hers. He pressed hard and her mouth opened in instant response. She gave a soft, gasping moan as his hands caressed each breast, his thumb slowly passing over each firm nipple, a finger circling the light pink areola.

"Aaaaah, uuuuuh," she groaned, and the groan became a moaning cry as his mouth left hers and found her breast, drew it in deeply, his tongue moving back and forth across the tip. "Aaaaaah . . . ah, yes, aaaaaah," Carol moaned, and small, low sounds rose from inside her. His hand rose from between her thighs, came to rest against the bottom of the dusty-blond triangle, and her long legs fell open, came together, fell open again. She was making deep, growling moans.

He touched and felt her already moist, the pathway smoothed, the welcome of the flesh that had grown damp. His maleness came down onto the dusty-blond triangle and he felt the pubic mound firm, risen to bear its own witness to ecstasy. Carol's long legs began to move slowly up and down his legs, against his waist and buttocks, and her torso began a sinuous, serpentine movement of its own. He heard the words emerge from the long, growling moans, "Yes . . . take me . . . oh, God . . . aaaaah . . . aaaah . . . take me . . . I want . . . oh, God I want." Her legs had begun to rub faster against him, her body now writhing and undulating. No fast, pumping motions for Carol. Everything a slow, serpentine twisting. Her hand came behind his neck and pulled his mouth down to her breasts. The long, low moans became a sudden half-scream as he slid quickly forward, into the wet portal.

Her legs clasped around him and rubbed up and down, long thighs caressing his hips and waist as her torso slowly undulated with his every thrusting pleasure. He felt himself swept up in her slow yet exciting motions that rubbed against him inside and outside, each one a little stronger, a little faster than the one before yet each retaining its serpentine excitement. Her hands pressed his mouth from one breast to the other and she groaned and moaned, all in a deep growling sound, scattered words somehow formed out of the rasping moan that was of itself strangely exciting.

Her long legs suddenly stretched out and rose up against him again, rubbed and caressed as her hips half-circled with a kind of slow haste that turned maddeningly exciting. He twisted with her, held in the serpent's coils, and her moans were growing deeper suddenly with new growling fervor. An almost terrible deep cry came from her, rising up, and her long legs locked behind the small of his back. He felt the long waves of ecstasy pulsating against him, contracting again and again. She was groaning and moaning as she tossed her dusty-blond hair from side to side. Her wet walls of sweet confinement pulled on him and he felt the world swept away as he sank deep inside her throbbing. His own groan of ecstasy mingled with her deep cries.

Her legs continued to rub against him after he felt the moment explode and vanish with despairing quickness. He heard her deep cry of protest. Her torso continued to undulate until it finally slowed, not unlike a top spinning down, and her harsh breaths wet his chest. He lay half atop her, and her arms and legs stayed tight around him until finally he felt her relax, her long thighs open and drop away as a flower unfolding. He shifted and lay beside her, his eyes on a level with the long curve of one breast. He lay quietly and waited for her to say something. But she said absolutely nothing, and when he rose onto one elbow to look at her, she turned to him, and he saw a kind of simmering wildness in the muted blue depths.

"I'll see to Annie," he said, and rose, naked but still warm in the steamy night. He changed the compress on Annie's forehead and felt her face and arms. She was still cool, he noted with satisfaction, and he returned to where Carol lay stretched on her back. Her long, willowy body seemed completely at home in this forest of sensuous fragrances and passionate colors. She looked up at him as he stood beside her. He saw her shoulders move and expected her arms to reach up for him. But her shoulders half-turned, moved back again, and as he watched, her waist and upper torso began to turn and twist, slow, writhing movements, her breasts swaying rhythmically with each twist. Her hips began to undulate slowly, her long thighs opening and closing, her legs moving up and down. Suddenly she was a twisting writhing incarnation of sheer sensuousness. He felt himself responding, his body expanding, and it was then that she reached up, her hand finding his pulsating warmth.

"Oh, yes, oh, yes, uuuuuuh," she moaned. She was slowly twisting, slowly writhing, long legs moving in erotic rhythm as she pulled him down onto her. Her hips lifted to take him in, and once again he was caught up in her slow, serpentine lovemaking. Not unlike a horizontal slow dance, he found himself reflecting as he swayed and twisted with her and felt the excitement of her long thighs rubbing against him. No words at all, only the deep, growling moans of utter ecstasy until finally the dusty-blond hair fell from side to side and he felt her contracting with him and around him. Her writhing never ceased as she came, only her long moans suddenly growing short, turning to low, gasped sounds, until the final groan of despair and protest, and she lay still beneath him.

When he finally slid from her relaxed, still, willowy body, she turned on her side, pushed herself up, and rested one breast against his mouth as she went to sleep without a single word. He lay awake, unable not to contrast Carol with Annie. Their passion had been so completely different, one all tempestuousness, the other all sinuousness, the flesh a mirror of the spirit. But as prophets, they were both right on target, and he could only admire that kind of ability. He closed his eyes and let himself nap till it was time to change Annie's compress again. He slid from Carol and she stayed asleep as he put a new cool towel on Annie and found that she felt normal. He ran his hands over her face and neck and chest and could feel no fever. He let himself embrace real hope for the first time as he returned to Carol and took a moment to enjoy the lovely sight of her willowy body before he settled down beside her. She half-turned, her arms around him at once, without waking.

He slept until daybreak woke him along with the raucous calls of brilliantly plumed parrots. He slid from Carol's arms, took his things to the little stream,

112

and washed and dressed. Carol was sitting up when he returned. He was walking toward Annie when he heard the soft moaning sound and saw her turn her head. He was beside Annie on one knee instantly as she moaned again and turned her head back. He saw her arms flex and she moved her legs, but her eyes were still closed. Carol slipped the nightgown on as she hurried over.

"She's coming around," Fargo said. "Hot damn, she's coming around."

Carol stayed beside him as he watched Annie move her head again, stretch her neck up and back. The sun had come up to cast its warm yellow blanket down when he saw Annie's eyelids move—slow, fluttering motions first, then her eyes came open, brown orbs staring up at him.

He reached out, cupping her face with his hands. "Welcome back," he said, and Annie's eyes focused on him and then she blinked. She started to push up on her elbows and he helped her sit up. She sat for a moment, shook her head. "How do you feel?" he asked.

"A little dizzy," Annie murmured.

"Stay there. Take it nice and slow," Fargo told her.

She leaned forward and put her head into his chest. "You made it. God, that's all I thought about while we were running," she murmured. She pulled her head back after a moment and her glance took in Carol. "The last thing I remember was hitting the branch."

"That was three nights ago," Carol said, and Annie looked aghast.

"Three nights ago?" she echoed. "What happened since?"

"You were in some kind of coma, with a high fever," Carol said. "I guess the concussion did it."

"I was afraid to move you. We kept putting cold compresses on you all day and night," Fargo said.

"Jeez." Annie frowned.

"You want to try standing?" Fargo asked.

Annie nodded and he pulled her to her feet. She swayed for a moment and held on to him until she finally relaxed her grip and stood alone. She took a tentative step, then another, stretched, and walked in a small circle.

"I was dizzy for a minute, but it's gone now," she said.

"How does the head feel?" Fargo questioned.

"It hurts a little, sort of a dull ache, but it's not too bad," Annie said. "I need to wash and do things."

"There's a stream through those laurels," Carol said, and Annie slowly walked to the light-brown horse and took her pack down. Fargo watched her closely as she walked into the trees and saw no signs of dizziness or unsteady steps.

"I think she's going to be fine," he said.

"I'll get changed," Carol said, and paused beside him, the muted blue eyes dancing. "I'm even more glad now that I took last night," she murmured.

"Me, too," he agreed, and she hurried away. Fargo spied some fruit nearby, used his knife to cut and taste it, and found it deliciously sweet. He unwrapped the remains of the rabbit from the leaves. Cold rabbit tasted as good as cold chicken, he knew, and he waited till Annie returned in a fresh shirt and looking amazingly fit. A touch of color had returned to her face, he saw. "Think you can eat?" he asked.

"God, yes. I feel empty inside," she said, and he watched her hungrily down the fruit and the cold rabbit.

"You up to riding?" he asked as Carol appeared, dressed, her usual coolly poised self.

"I'm sure of it," Annie said. "Hell, we've lost three days."

"Let's give it a try," Fargo said, and watched from the Ovaro as she climbed into the saddle without difficulty. He set a slow pace, nonetheless, and continued following the narrow passages southward that snaked through the forest. He called frequent halts and Annie's rueful smile held gratitude as she stretched out at every rest. But she grew visibly stronger as the day wore on, and by late afternoon she appeared to be her usual pert self. However, when the day drew to an end, he noted that she was very willing to sleep. Carol lay down on her sheet without wrapping it around herself, a small gesture to the death of modesty, he smiled.

But he had other concerns pressing on his mind, concerns that had been growing as they rode through the day. So far the search had been trailless and fruitless. He had followed the paths that had opened in the dense forest. They seemed likely ones any fugitives would take rather than fight their way through the almost impenetrable foliage. Yet he'd found nothing, no signs, prints, markings. Even the stealthy Seminoles couldn't transport a half-dozen young girls without leaving signs. The riddle stayed with him until he drew sleep around himself, certain there had to be an answer.

7

Annie seemed very much herself when morning came, and he waited until he called the first halt of the day to face both her and Carol. "Something's wrong," he said flatly. "Nobody's going to find their way through this place without some kind of trail, and we haven't seen a damn sign."

"The Seminole could," Annie said.

"Even they would have to pick and poke their way and they couldn't move that slowly with captives. Split up into small groups, they have to follow some kind of trail," Fargo said. "Either I'm missing something or there's some other way through this forest that forms a trail. From here on we go real slow. I want to look at every damn tree."

"Whatever you say, Fargo." Annie shrugged and came alongside him as he swung onto the Ovaro while Carol drew up behind. He kept the horse at a walk and his gaze moved over the low branches and young twigs of every tree they passed as he searched for some sign or mark that might tell him something. Fifteen minutes had passed in the slow march when he reined to a halt in front of the tree with the light-gray bark tinged with pink. He frowned at the V-shaped mark that had been cut into one of the pink streaks on the bark.

"This is a tamarind, right?" he said to Annie, and she nodded. He dismounted and walked to the next

116

tree, a tall cotton gum. It was unmarked. So were the new two laurel oaks. A tupelo bore no marks, either. None of the trees near the tamarind were marked in any way, and he swore under his breath. Was the V cut into the tamarind a meaningless mark, done by some passing Seminole? He let his eyes scan the trees that stretched down the narrow passage and a dozen yards away he spotted another with the distinctive pink-tinged bark. Something stirred inside him and the frown crossed his forehead. He brushed past the other trees along the path, tossing a cursory glance at each, and came to a halt at the tamarind.

He felt the excitement bubble up inside him. Another V had been cut into the pink-tinged bark, and he motioned to Annie and Carol. They rode toward him at once, Annie leading the Ovaro. As they halted and stared at the mark, Fargo's eyes were already searching the trees ahead until he spotted another tamarind some thirty yards farther on. He climbed onto the pinto, and Carol and Annie followed him to the tree where he couldn't keep the triumph out of his voice as he saw the mark on it.

"That's it, dammit. The only trees they've marked are the tamarinds. It's a tamarind trail," he said.

"Clever," Carol commented. "Very few people would find it."

"Let's ride," Fargo said, and set off for the next tamarind some dozen yards away. The mark was there and his eyes searched for the next pink-tinged trunk. The tamarinds were spaced unevenly, some only a few yards apart, some almost fifty yards from each other. But each carried the V cut into the bark. The trees appeared on both sides of the narrow path. They had followed the trail for a good part of the day when Fargo reined to a sharp halt as he stared at the tamarind. The tree bore no mark.

"What happened? What's it mean?" Annie asked.

Fargo turned thoughts in his mind before answering. "It means we missed a turn," he said, wheeled the pinto around, and returned to the last tree with the V cut into it. He peered into the thick foliage of the forest. "They left the path here," he said, and began to push his way through the trees. He rode slowly, his eyes sweeping the denseness of the forest, and he was beginning to think he'd best turn back and explore the other side of the path when he spotted the tamarind. He made for the tree, picking his way around the closely packed forest giants, and heard his sigh of relief as he saw the mark cut into the tamarind. "The trail cuts through the thick of the Ocala from here," Fargo said.

"I wonder why it left the path." Carol frowned.

"The path goes someplace. I'm guessing this trail leads to nowhere," Fargo said.

"Nowhere?" Carol echoed.

"Nowhere, meaning someplace really secret, someplace no path goes to," Fargo said. "Only we're going to go there." His eyes went skyward through the almost-blanketing overhanging foliage. "It'll be dark soon. We'll bed down right here," he said, and dismounted.

Annie slid from her horse and came to him, admiration frank in her eyes. "You're something special," she said, and a sudden smile was made of a very private message. She turned away and began to take her things from her saddlepack.

Fargo found a spot to lay down in the dim dusk, a bed of thick panicgrass that offered a welcome mat to tired bones. He was starting to pull off clothes when Carol appeared beside him.

"I trust you haven't forgotten that you're also supposed to be looking for James Raynall," she said. "I see only chasing after Annie's cousin."

"I haven't forgotten, and I've been looking for signs

of him, too," Fargo said. "But this trail has become hot."

Carol rested a hand against his chest. "And I haven't changed my mind about what I said to you a few days ago," she murmured.

"What was that?" he asked.

"Little Annie still wants you," she said, the hint of amused warning in her tone. It was time for careful answers, he told himself.

"Wanting's one thing. Having's another," he said.

Carol's little smile was made of smugness. "Indeed," she said. "Poor little thing would have a fit if she knew." Carol brushed his cheek with a quick kiss and hurried off to change.

Fargo finished undressing and lay down. The answer had satisfied her. He'd be grateful for small favors. And keeping the truth to himself would be one more. He slept quickly and didn't wake till morning. He dressed, saddled the pinto as Carol woke, changed, and returned to offer him some fruit. She clung to his arm for a moment until Annie stirred and sat up. Fargo waited till Annie was ready to ride, and led the way through the thick foliage of the forest, finding the tamarinds among the densely packed trees.

Carol fell back some, having her troubles with the steamy heat and the hanging vines, and Annie swung beside Fargo at a small stretch of relative openness. "Carol's getting friendlier, isn't she?" Annie remarked, and he gave her a glance of mild surprise. "I saw her this morning when she thought I was still asleep," Annie explained.

"She's softened some. I think it was her close call with the forest people," Fargo said.

"She's still looking at you the same way. She still wants you," Annie said.

Fargo paused. A good answer deserved being used again, he told himself. "Wanting's one thing. Having's another," he said, and Annie returned a Cheshire-cat smile.

"So it is, and we know who's done the having, don't we?" she murmured.

"We sure do," Fargo said, and let himself sound conspiratorial. Annie fell silent as Carol caught up, but her pleased little smile stayed. He tried to increase the pace through the forest fastness with only partial success, but it was near midday when he halted where a small circle of cleared space suddenly appeared. He dismounted and scanned the ground. A grim smile came to his lips. "They came together here," he said. "Separate groups of prints, none really clear but enough to see. They joined up here and slept the night." He pointed to patches of the grass still flattened. Smaller marks were still visible in different places. "Shoes. The others were barefoot. Seminoles, Garson's men, and the girls, each leaving different marks."

"Why didn't we see any along the passages?" Carol asked.

"None of them took the passages until they reached the marked tamarinds," Fargo said. "We're not far behind. I'd guess we could catch up by day's end."

"Let's go," Annie said, excitement curled in her voice.

"Single-file, but stay close together," Fargo said as he mounted and led the way forward, his eyes still picking out the tamarinds that showed the way through the forest.

It was perhaps an hour later, the forest not quite so dense as it had been, though still deep and thick, that he caught sight of the darting figures that moved through the trees on both sides of them. He watched out of his peripheral vision, not turning his head, and saw the figures continued to stay alongside, darting from tree to tree in small cluster of three or four. He

motioned to Annie and Carol and they came alongside. "Keep your eyes forward," he said. "Don't look
around, but we've got company."

He heard both their breaths suck in sharply and
Carol forced herself not to automatically turn her
head. "Who?" she asked.

"Seminoles," Fargo said. "They're just moving
along with us, for now."

"Meaning you think they'll do more than that?"
Carol asked.

"Maybe. I'm not going to start any shooting unless
there's no other choice," Fargo said. "We just go on
nice and easy." He spotted another tamarind, slowed,
saw the mark cut into it, and moved on to the next.
The darting figures continued to parallel their progress, but he suddenly noticed they had come closer,
no longer trying to stay unseen. He wondered how
long they had been with them before he noticed their
presence. The forest began to become less dense and
the Seminoles were clear now. They were lithe figures,
wearing only loincloths, a shade more brown than the
plains tribes and smaller in stature.

But they moved with silent gracefulness, he noted,
almost seeming to glide through the trees. He shot a
glance at Carol and saw the nervousness in her face.
Annie's normal pugnaciousness masked any nervousness
she might have as she rode with her head held high,
her jaw set firmly. Suddenly Fargo saw the Seminoles
move in still closer, coming in only a few yards away
on both sides. Most carried small bows and all carried
knives, he noted. He thought about drawing the rifle
and decided against it as they still made no move to
do anything but run alongside. The last tamarind
appeared, the mark on it, and beyond the tree he saw
the forest open up. As the trees spread out the ground
seemed to drop off and he suddenly found himself

past the last line of trees and reining to a halt at a ledge.

The land sloped downward into a kind of wide, cleared area, and as Annie and Carol halted alongside him, he saw the Seminoles also come to a halt. Fargo stared down at a scene that might have been a page of history turned back. A community lay spread out before him that made him think of pictures he had once seen of the ancient Incan civilizations.

The entire community was contained in a large square tract of cleared land. At one side the land bordered on a large lake while the other three sides were rimmed with forest. Fargo counted some thirty tepees along one edge of the square and six wooden huts along the adjoining side. In the very center of the tract a stone circle of some half-dozen steps led to a log hut with a thatched roof. Directly in front of the hut a stone, thronelike structure rested. Fargo's eyes moved across the main part of the area where he saw rows of growing things: corn, squash, beans, guava, lettuce, onions, and potatoes, along with a few vegetables he didn't recognize.

Indian women, bare-breasted and wearing small skirtlike garments from the waist to their knees, were busy at work at stone mills, pounding and grinding seeds while youngsters, mostly naked, filled huge baskets with shucked corn. But perhaps most impressive of all were the long irrigation trenches and raised sluices that carried water from the lake to almost every section of the tract. He also noted treadmill pumps to keep the water running when the natural flow weakened. Fargo's eyes went to the large lake again. Its shore made up the entire length of one side of the tract. Two wood huts had been built a dozen feet from the shore, their closed doors facing the community. The only jarring note in the otherwise busy, peaceful community were the four Indians, each with rifle in hand, who stood outside the two huts, plainly serving as guards.

"The whole place has been carved out of the forest," Fargo heard Carol murmur, her voice echoing his own awe.

"And made into a self-sufficient community," Fargo said.

"Hardly seems the place for selling stolen girls," Carol said with a trace of waspishness. "I think you've been chasing the wrong trail."

Annie said nothing, but the tightness of her lips told Fargo that she recognized the very distinct possibility in Carol's words.

"We know the Seminoles were involved somehow, and this is a Seminole community," Fargo said. "I'm not writing off anything yet." His glances went to the guards in front of the two huts and suddenly six of the Seminoles alongside them stepped forward and one gestured with his hands. "We're being invited down," Fargo said.

"I'd say invited isn't exactly the right word," Annie muttered. He grunted agreement as he nosed the Ovaro down the shallow slope. Annie and Carol followed a few paces behind him, and as he reached the level land and rode through the tract, he saw all work come to a halt as men, women, and children watched the three new arrivals. The two rows of Seminole warriors still moved alongside them, Fargo noted, and they steered him toward the half-circle of stone steps. They halted when they reached the lowest step and Fargo's eyes swept the tract of land as other men and women came in closer.

"You speak Seminole?" Carol asked him.

"No, but I'm good at sign language," Fargo said.

More of the Indians had come in front, their tasks to form a half-circle around them, staring up at the intruders with expressionless faces.

123

"What are they waiting for?" Carol muttered.

"You might be about to get an answer," Fargo said as he saw the door of the wood hut atop the raised stone circle open. A man strode into the open, a white man, handsome with grayish hair, a straight nose, and a strong jaw. Gray-blue eyes looked down at them with imperiousness. He was bare-chested, clad only in trousers, and he wore a star-shaped gleaming gold medallion on a chain of beads from around his neck.

"My God," Fargo heard Carol breathe and cast a glance at her. She was staring openmouthed up at the man. "It's James. It's Raynall," she gasped.

Fargo returned his gaze to the figure at the top of the steps and saw the man frowning down at them. He gestured with one hand and the Seminole motioned for Fargo to mount the steps. Fargo swung from the saddle and Annie and Carol did the same. They were beside him as he started to climb the half-dozen stone steps. "Are you sure?" he murmured to Carol out of the side of his mouth.

"Yes, I'm sure," she hissed. "My God, I don't understand any of this."

Fargo saw the man sit down on the stone thronelike seat and continue to regard them with an imperious frown until they reached the top. His gray-blue eyes paused at Fargo and Annie and focused on Carol. The frown on his face deepened. "Carol Siebert. Is that really you?" he asked in a deep, sonorous voice.

"Yes, it is, James," Carol said. "My God, what is all this about? What are you doing here in that outfit?"

James Raynall stood up, stretched his arms out with benevolent majesty as he advanced on Carol. She stepped forward and let him embrace her until she pulled back.

"Who are these people with you, Carol?" James Raynall asked, and his eyes went to Fargo.

"That's Skye Fargo. I hired him to find you," Carol said.

Raynall let his eyes stay on the big man. "He did. He must be very good," Raynall said. "He's the only one that ever has."

"That's why they call him the Trailsman," Carol said, and saw Raynall's eyes flick to Annie. "That's Annie Dowd. She's with us, but she was looking for something else."

"I see," Raynall said, and fastened Annie with an appraising glance before turning his attention back to Carol. "We've a lot to talk about, Carol," he beamed. "You and your friends will be my guests for dinner. We'll make it a festive occasion, a feast for our reunion."

"We indeed do have a lot to talk about, James," Carol said, and Raynall pulled her to him with an arm around her waist.

"You are as lovely as ever, my dear. You were the only one that tried to understand me," he said.

"I don't understand any of this," Carol said, gesturing to the crowd watching and the community. "Where do you fit in here, James?"

"All in time, my dear, all in time," Raynall said, and turned to walk down the stone steps.

Fargo watched as everyone bowed in obeisance, some of the Indian women dropping to their knees. He caught a glimpse of a young girl, dark-haired but very definitely not a Seminole. Raynall spoke to the Seminoles in their language, his voice magisterial, and Fargo saw the tension leave the crowd. They rose to their feet at a sign from Raynall and moved away, suddenly chattering excitedly among themselves.

Raynall returned to the top of the circular steps and lowered himself onto the thronelike stone seat, his handsome face wreathed in benevolent contentment. "Where'd you learn Seminole?" Fargo asked.

"Right here, from the Indians, and I've taught some to speak a little English," Raynall said. "We will feast tonight, on the wild pig that roams this region, a tasty dish."

"James, what is this all about? What are you doing here? Why haven't you let us hear from you?" Carol asked with an edge of reproach.

Raynall swept one arm out in an encompassing gesture. "These are my children, my people," he said.

"This is a Seminole Indian tribe," Fargo cut in, and drew a chiding smile.

"This is a people reborn," Raynall said. "Everything you see here I taught them to build. I taught them how to irrigate their land and plant their crops, how to build wooden shovels with which to dig the trenches, how to construct pumps to keep the water running. And I taught them, showed them, gave them the gift of my engineering knowledge. A civilization has been created here."

"It seems tremendous, James," Carol said. "But how did it begin?"

"I was searching when I came upon the Seminole. They were hostile at first, but I showed them I was a friend. I showed them little things, at first: how to build wood shovels with which to dig, how to run water through an irrigation trench for just a few feet, then for yards, and so on. I wanted to learn their tongue so I could teach them more, and soon I was able to teach them all the things they now know," Raynall said.

"It was a challenge. You always liked challenges," Carol said.

"At first, and then it became more than that. It became a kind of happiness and satisfaction I'd never felt before," Raynall said.

"Obviously," Carol said. "But we have to talk more

about so many things, your going back with me being one of them."

Raynall's smile was made of a kind of tolerant pity. "Going back?" he echoed. "Carol, my dear, I'm not going back."

Fargo watched the disbelief flood Carol's face. "You can't be serious. You can't really think of staying here," she said.

"Does one turn away from paradise?" Raynall asked her with another tolerant smile. Carol stared at him, speechless for a moment. "I have everything a man could want here, my dear," Raynall went on. "Peace, pleasure, all the simple satisfactions for the mind, the spirit, and the body." He paused, studied Carol for a moment. "You find that hard to believe, of course."

"Yes." Carol nodded. "Maybe you've done wonderful things here, James, but these are primitive people. You are a man of intellect. How can you be happy here?"

"Precisely because I am a man of intellect, my dear," Raynall answered. "I can see what ordinary men cannot see. Most people spend all their lives working and struggling to acquire riches of cash or land. Some do it out of greed. Some for power, but most so that they will one day be able to enjoy all the simple gifts of peace and comfort. Only by that time most are too old to really enjoy what they have achieved. These people enjoy that peace and comfort now, every day and every night. They have no need to struggle. They have no need for greed or power. I ask you, my dear, who are the primitive ones?"

"I guess people have different ideas of what's happiness and what's primitive," Annie said brusquely.

Her tone didn't ruffle Raynall, Fargo noted as the man bestowed a calm glance at her. "I have learned as well as taught since coming here. Perhaps you have a lot more learning to do, young woman," he said.

"Maybe, but I can see and it seems to me they look at you as some sort of God sent them by the great spirit," Annie said.

"Perhaps, in a way, I am that," he said. "Why did I come this way instead of another? Perhaps because it was meant to be. Fate guides our destinies."

"James, we have to talk more about all this, just the two of us," Carol cut in.

"Of course. There'll be plenty of time for that. Right now, I will rest before our festive dinner. I'll put the three of you in one of our extra huts so you may do the same thing. Rest before dinner is as important as afterward. The digestive juices do not work properly on a tired stomach," Raynall said, and rose to his feet, gesturing with a regal motion for them to follow as he went down the steps.

When he reached the bottom, three young, bare-breasted maidens came up to Raynall, each carrying a small bowl of oil and with a towel over each arm. Fargo saw long wooden tables being set out while white sheets were placed over them to serve as table-cloths. An older woman stood by with a small cart filled with more sheets, and Fargo felt the frown dig into his brow. Raynall nodded to the three young maidens. "My daily massage," he said.

"Very nice," Fargo said as his eyes swept the square tract of land. "You have spinning wheels someplace?" he asked.

Raynall's eyes held a moment of admiration. "The sheets, correct?" he asked, and Fargo nodded. "You indeed have an observant eye, Fargo," the man said.

"Occupational habit," Fargo remarked.

"No, I do not have spinning wheels. I haven't attempted the teaching of that yet, and I'm not sure we could find the material with which to work here,"

Raynall said. "The sheets are brought to me by my one contact with the outside world, an indulgence you might say. They are brought by a gentleman who is also my guest at the moment. You'll meet him tonight." He turned and spoke to one of the Seminole men, and Fargo followed the Indian to one of the wood huts with Carol and Annie. Inside, the hut turned out to be one large room with a narrow window and candles burning in stone holders to furnish light.

A row of sheets were stacked in one corner of the room and rattan mats were loosely strewn on the floor. Annie lowered herself onto one of them. "This is sure a surprise. We think we're following the girls and we find Raynall," she said.

"We were following the girls. We were on the right trail, from what Azard told us," Fargo said.

"Then why is it Raynall we found?" Annie questioned.

"I don't know. Not yet, anyway," Fargo said with a frown, and turned to Carol. "You've learned one thing: Raynall's alive," he said, and Carol nodded.

"But he's not going back with you," Annie sniffed.

"Of course he is," Carol said sharply. "He's just all caught up in what he's done here. Wait till I talk to him alone."

"Won't matter any. He's gone off the deep end," Annie said.

Carol shot a glance at Fargo that begged support. "You're both right, but the bottom line is that he's a king here, an emperor. Few men will walk away from what he has here. Face it, how often does an engineer become a king? How often does a businessman get to be an emperor? Everything for the mind, the spirit, and the body was how he put it. That translates to power, comfort, and sex," Fargo said.

"Sex?" Carol frowned.

"Don't be naïve, honey. I'm sure he has any woman he wants here," Fargo said. "I'm just not sure how far he carries this emperor thing."

"He'll listen to me. He always has. You'll see," Carol insisted, and Fargo sat down on one of the mats.

"Good luck," he said, and stretched out. "Meanwhile, I'll take his advice and get in a nap." He closed his eyes and drew sleep to himself, dimly hearing Annie toss and turn. When he woke later, he saw Carol sitting, knees drawn up, her face grave. Two young Seminole girls, not more than twelve, he guessed, with little, immature breasts and slender bodies, entered with stone basins with water and carrying towels. They silently left and Fargo let Annie and Carol freshen up first and followed them from the hut when he finished.

In the remaining light of the dusk, he saw the tables, each covered with the white sheets that served as tablecloths, were heaped high with fruits and vegetables. A fire blazed in a long pit where the pig had been cut into small sections so it would roast more quickly. The flavorful odor hanging in the air told him the roast was almost done. Long torches were lighted as night descended to illuminate the scene. He saw Raynall at the center table beckon to him. The man was still bare-chested, but a red sash crossed his chest under the gleaming medallion.

"Please sit, you here beside me, Carol," Raynall said, and Carol lowered herself onto the long wood bench at his right.

Fargo sat beside her with Annie next to him. The fruit looked delicious and the taste matched its appearance.

"I'm not hungry," Annie muttered.

"Eat, dammit. No sulking," Fargo growled, and she pouted but obeyed. Steaming corn was brought to the table by Seminoles, who served as waiters, and Fargo spied the three men emerge from one of the nearby huts and walk toward the table. He felt Annie stiffen beside him and caught her sharp gasp as she recognized the approaching figure.

"It's Garson," she breathed.

"Yes," Fargo agreed, and Annie was on her feet instantly.

"What's he doing here?" she barked at Raynall.

"Do you know Max?" Raynall asked.

"I sure do know that stinking polecat," Annie snapped.

Raynall fastened her with a severe glance. "Max Garson is a friend as well as a guest. I will not have my guests insulted, young woman," he said.

Fargo tugged at Annie's arm. "Sit down," he whispered, but Annie's temper, always close to the surface, had exploded.

"Don't tell me what to say, mister," she flung back. "I asked you what's he doing here?"

"Max Garson is my contact with the outside world. I value my relationship with him. He supplies me with the sheets and towels we have so much use for and sometimes with rolls of bandages and other medical supplies. I give him the use of some of my best hunters for his good work."

"Good work? What good work?" Annie frowned.

"Max rescues young girls who are abused, mistreated, used as slaves, often beaten and starved, poor, miserable young women who need to be rescued from where they are," Raynall said.

"That's a crock of shit," Annie shouted. "He takes girls from perfectly good homes and sells them to whorehouses or rich men who want their own playtoys. That's why he takes only young girls. That's why I hired Fargo to chase after him."

Raynall turned his gaze on Max Garson, who offered a tolerant smile. "James, she's lying through

131

her teeth, except for the part about chasing after me. She's kin to one of the young women I took. She won't admit the girl needed saving," Garson said calmly.

Raynall turned his glance to Annie. "Is that true? Are you kin to one of those poor girls?"

"Yes, but that's got nothing to do with anything," Annie returned.

"I'd say it certainly has," Raynall said, turning to Fargo. "Did this young woman hire you to track the girls?"

"She did," Fargo admitted.

Raynall turned to Carol with a frown. "But you told me you hired Fargo to find me, Carol," he said.

"I did, but she insisted on hiring him also," Carol said.

"What do you know about the things she's been saying here?" Raynall persisted.

"Only that she's said them right along. I can't say whether they're true or not," Carol answered.

Fargo caught Annie's glare at him. "You know he tried to keep me from following you. He tried to kill me. Say something," she snapped.

"I know he tried to stop you. And I know the reasons you gave me. I can't swear to more than that," Fargo said, and watched the shock pass through her face.

"Damn you, Fargo," she spit out, spun on her heel, and strode from the table.

Fargo and the others watched her storm into the hut and slam the door behind her.

"There's a young woman in need of manners and discipline," Raynall said.

"She's not only a liar, she's dangerous, James," Max Garson said.

"I'll see to her," Fargo put in, and sat down again.

Raynall accepted the remark and lowered himself

down beside Carol once more. Garson took a seat at the table, his two men flanking him, and began to eat as the roast was served.

"We still must talk, James, just you and I," Carol told Raynall.

"Tomorrow, my dear. There'll be plenty of time," Raynall said.

"Tell me, what happens to these girls that are rescued?" Fargo asked, keeping his tone casual. "Your men take them for Garson. They bring them here, right?"

"Yes, to clean them and give them a chance to rest," Raynall said. "Then Max takes them east to the coast, near New Smyrna. The people who will give them good and proper homes meet them there, people Max has investigated beforehand."

"The last group, have they been sent on yet?" Fargo asked, still keeping his voice casual, but he saw the quick exchange of glances between Garson and Raynall.

"Yes, they have," Raynall said. "But enough of such serious conversation. Let's eat and be merry."

"Why not?" Fargo nodded and dug into the roast with enthusiasm.

Raynall held the conversation to stories about all he had done with the Seminoles and held some reminiscences with Carol. Fargo watched her and saw she tried to be charming and attentive, but the tiny lines of tightness around her mouth revealed her inner nervousness. When the evening ended, Raynall gestured to some of the servers, who immediately began to take away the remaining food. Fargo rescued a piece of the roast and held it up to Raynall with a smile. "For my unmannerly little friend," he said. "I don't favor starvation as a way to teach manners."

"No, of course not. I hope you sleep well." Raynall smiled and took Carol's hand when she rose with him.

"We'll have a lot to talk about tomorrow. I'll enjoy showing you how beautiful life is here in this little paradise I've fashioned for these good people." He kissed her on the cheek and stepped back. As he climbed the circle of stone steps to his hut, Fargo saw the Seminoles bow down. He took Carol's arm and started for the hut that had been assigned to them. He paused as he passed Garson. The man's eyes had grown hard.

"You keep that little bitch quiet and maybe you can all stay alive," Garson said.

"I never argue with a man who has the upper hand," Fargo said, and moved on. Before entering the hut, he looked back, his eyes sweeping the area still lighted by the dying fire and the torches, and he found what he sought. The three horses had been tethered to one side where a pole rose from alongside a row of corn. The candles still burned inside the hut as he entered, and Annie, seated cross-legged on one of the mats, looked up with fury in her pert face. "Get out. Find someplace else to sleep," she spit at him. "I don't want you here."

"First, that's not your decision. Second, simmer down," Fargo said.

"Simmer down? You've your dammed nerve saying that to me after you as much as agreed with Garson," she said, and waved a hand at Carol. "I can understand her. She doesn't really know more than what I told her. But you do. You know he tried to burn me out and kill me."

"I know that. I didn't want to take your side, not then, not yet," Fargo said. "We need more time and I bought some tonight."

"The girls are here, aren't they?" Annie said. "You said you were sure we were following the right trail. That's what you meant. Why were you suspicious?"

"The guards in front of those two huts," Fargo said.

"And I know something more now, too. Raynall's involved in his own way. The Seminole aren't working for Garson. I was right about that. They're going along with him because Raynall wants them to."

"Are you saying that James is involved in the stealing and selling of girls?" Carol put in. "I can't believe that."

"Maybe not the same way Garson is, but he's involved. Garson brings him the things he wants and he supplies the Seminoles to do the job for Garson. He looks the other way. It suits him to believe Garson's story about rescuing girls," Fargo said.

"Maybe he does believe it," Carol said.

"Bullshit. He's a maniac, a self-made emperor. I'll bet he's had a few of Garson's girls for himself before they're sent on," Fargo said.

Carol stared into space for a long moment, emotions whirling through her, the muted-blue eyes darkened with confusion. "Look, if you're right, maybe I can end it all," she said finally. "I still think I can convince James to go back with me. If I can, I'm sure he'll let the girls go."

"You think Garson will stand around for that?" Annie asked.

"Will he have much choice? James could have him killed in an instant," Carol said.

"You're right about that part and wrong about the rest," Fargo said. "He's not going back with you and he's not letting you go back. Nor any of us."

"Of course he'll let me go back," Carol protested.

"No way, honey. I've watched him look at you. He's thinking about making you his top woman here, his version of a queen," Fargo said.

"You're wrong. I'll prove it tomorrow," Carol said.

"Good luck. But you talk to him about his going back. Nothing else, understand?" Fargo said, his voice growing harsh. Carol nodded and lay down on one of the mats as Fargo tossed the piece of roast at Annie. "Eat. You're going to need all your strength," he said.

Annie nodded and bit into the piece of meat.

"Please blow out the candles," Carol said, and he quickly plunged the hut into blackness. He undressed and lay awake as he let one plan after another drift through his mind. He considered each, rejected most, finally settled on two possible actions that might succeed. The odds on both would be rejected by any gambling man, he knew as he went to sleep.

8

When dawn found its way into the hut, Fargo woke and glanced across at Annie and Carol. Both had shed clothes entirely in the heat of the almost airless hut. Carol lay on her back, one long lovely leg bent, her willowy body as beautiful as a nodding trillium. Annie lay on her side, legs half-drawn up, her high, round breasts and compact body lovely as an orange milk-weed about to burst open. The beauty of contrast, he sighed as he tiptoed from the cabin. He dressed and washed outside and sat down and watched the commu-nity come awake.

Raynall's hut remained silent as Annie and Carol finally emerged and walked quietly beside him. Two Seminole women came up with bowls of fruit that made a delicious breakfast. Fargo strolled past the two huts where the four Seminole stood guard. The Indi-ans watched him go by with only passing interest, he noted. He moved on to the edge of the lake, where it began a long curve. "If the girls are in there, why are they only guarding the front of the lake?" Carol asked. "Anyone could swim up from behind."

Annie made a derisive sound and Fargo pointed to the plantlife that grew in the water all along the shore-line where the huts were.

"Sawgrass," he said. "It cuts worse than a razor blade. That's better than any guards they could put out. Nobody will swim through it and live, except a gator. The girls are in those huts." He smiled grimly as, when they strolled on, he saw four women bring food and water into the two huts. He also glimpsed Max Garson watching them from the doorway of his hut. Raynall appeared and strode to the thronelike seat at the top of the steps. Fargo watched the Seminoles bow down in greeting. "Emperor Raynall," Fargo muttered.

Annie's voice held despair in it for the first time. "We'll never do it. We can't get them away from all this. Maybe if we only had Garson to fight, but not this whole damn community," she said.

"There's a way, and it's our only chance, for ourselves as well as the girls," Fargo said.

"I'll convince James to go back with us. That'll put an end to everything," Carol said. She stepped away from him and walked out to meet Raynall as he came down the steps. He took her arm and led her back to his hut followed by two young girls bearing breakfast.

"Hell, maybe she can pull it off," Annie said.

"I'm not big on miracles," Fargo said. "It's time to make some plans." He led her to a place not far from where the horses were tethered, sat down, and motioned for her to do the same. He stretched out on one elbow, pulled a blade of grass from the ground, and idly chewed on it.

"You sure seem awful cool and calm for someone who's not big on miracles," Annie remarked.

"That's the idea. Garson's watching us," Fargo said. "Stretch out and relax while you listen real carefully. You're right, we'll never get those girls away with Raynall's Seminoles after us. That means we have to keep them from going after us."

"How in hell do you expect to do that?" Annie asked as she lay on her back, not looking at him.

"Raynall's going to do that for us," Fargo said, and

she turned her head to stare at him for a moment. "They'll do whatever he tells them to do."

"And he's going to tell them to let us walk away with the girls?" Annie frowned.

"He's a king, but even kings like to live," Fargo said. "That's where you come in. You're going to go to him tonight. You'll be sweet. You'll apologize for last night. You'll tell him how you might like to stay here. You'll make it plain that you'd welcome a roll in the hay with him."

"What if he takes me up on it? He just might, you know."

"He'll be relaxed, off-guard and horny. You know how to use that six-gun of yours. No shooting, though. Just knock him out and wait for me."

"Where are you going to be?" Annie frowned.

"Getting the girls out," he said.

"You said that was impossible. The guards in front and the sawgrass behind."

"I've an idea that might just work. I'll find out the hard way tonight," he said.

Annie tossed him a sidelong glance with her eyes growing narrow. "Why me with Raynall? Why not Carol? You said he's got his eye on her."

"Because he's known her too long. He knows she's not the kind to suddenly make a play for him. He'd get suspicious. But he won't with you. He'll figure you're being smart enough to make the best of a bad situation."

Annie considered the answer for a moment. "All right," she said finally, and her hand stole into his. She lay quietly beside him under the warm sun and didn't speak until he sat up when the sun passed the noon sky. "What if your idea doesn't work tonight?" she asked.

"You're on your own, honey," Fargo said, and pulled her to her feet. He walked to the hut with her, and young girls brought corn and cooked beans for lunch along with pieces of papaya. He accepted the food and ate inside the hut with Annie. When they finished, the girls returned for the bowls and left fresh water. He stepped outside after they left, Annie at his heels, and surveyed the lay of the lake again, the bed of sawgrass and the line of trees that bordered the far side of the tract. He stayed beside the hut and Annie did the same. It was midafternoon when Carol emerged from Raynall's hut to slowly walk down the stone steps.

He watched her come toward him and saw the tightness in her face. He followed her into the hut, Annie at his heels, and she turned to him, her lips quivering. "You were right, about all of it," she bit out. "He won't go back and he told me I was going to stay, too."

"As his queen," Fargo said.

"Something like that. Chief wife might be more appropriate," Carol said. "He didn't ask if I'd stay, no subtlety at all. He just told me I was staying."

"Emperors don't need to ask," Fargo said.

Carol's hands twisted around each other and there was shocked acceptance mixed with the despair in his voice. "He is mad, drunk with himself and his power here. You were right about that, too," she said. "He wants to see you."

Fargo nodded, unsurprised at the request, and started for the door. "Can't keep a king waiting," he said. He passed Max Garson and his two cronies on his way to Raynall. Garson regarded him with the half-amused expression of a man totally in control of his intended victim. Raynall met him at the door of the hut and offered an expansive smile.

"I was very impressed by your abilities in finding me," the man said. "I wonder if you might do some work for me here. I'm thinking of expanding our community southward. I'll like you to take ten of the Seminoles and explore the forest for the best way to clear new land, the areas least difficult with trails we can use for bringing tools and supplies."

"Sounds all right to me," Fargo said.

"Wonderful. Then you could start tomorrow," Raynall beamed.

"Why not?" Fargo agreed, and walked out of the hut. He kept the grim smile inside himself going down the stone steps. Raynall was lying, of course. He'd no plans to expand. He'd no reason for it. He had all he wanted neatly contained in the community as it was. The work offer was simply an excuse to get him away from here while Garson spirited the girls out. Once that was done, his life wouldn't be worth a plugged nickel, Fargo knew. But Raynall believed he had accepted the offer, and that's all he wanted for now, one more night.

The day was beginning to drift to an end when he returned to the hut where Carol and Annie waited. "He offered me a job." Fargo grinned. "Finding new trails south from here."

"What'd you say?" Annie asked.

"I took it," Fargo said. "I expect not to show up for work, come morning." He met Carol's eyes and saw the pain still in their muted blue depths. "He invited you to eat with him alone tonight, didn't he?"

"Yes," she said.

"Two important things. One, tell him you and Annie both want sheets for sleeping, two each. He'll give them to you. Second, beg off early. Annie's going to visit him after you leave."

Carol frowned as she nodded. "What's going on?"

"I'm going to try to get us all out of here with the girls," Fargo said, and she looked at him in disbelief. "Annie will fill you in on some of it. I'll finish the rest later," he said, and went outside.

His eyes swept the tract of land again, in the day's last light. A new set of four guards had replaced the others in front of the two huts, he noted. He saw Garson and his men filling their packs with fruit and cooked vegetables. They were preparing for their trip to the coast tomorrow, and he felt his lips draw back tightly. His plans for getting to the girls were set. So were his plans for handling Raynall. But Garson remained the problem. It was one he'd have to somehow handle when confronted with it, come morning, and he turned back into the hut as night descended.

Carol had changed and was about to go to Raynall. "Be nice. Tell him the idea of staying is appealing more to you, and get those sheets," Fargo told her. She hurried outside with a nod and two young girls appeared with dinner. "He's such a considerate host," Fargo said, and lay down after the girls took the bowls back. He napped, Annie beside him, until he heard Carol's footsteps returning. She put the sheets down as she sank onto a mat, a terrible sadness in her face.

"He's so different from the man I knew," she murmured. "So completely different. I faked being very tired. That's how I got away. Otherwise, I think he'd have tried to take me."

Fargo nodded to Annie. "Good. He'll be ripe and ready for your visit," he said. "Get moving."

Annie rose and hurried from the hut and Fargo went to the door and peered out. The community was still and no figures moved under an almost full moon.

He turned inside the hut again and undressed down to his drawers, gun belt, and the calf holster. "You stay here," he said to Carol. "You've done your part for now. You'll have more to do when I get back."

He picked up the sheets, folded them over one arm, and hurried from the hut at a crouching lope. He crossed through the center of the sleeping community and made for the curve of the lakeshore. When he reached it, he took one of the sheets and began to wrap it tightly around one leg. He wrapped it thickly and, finally finished, tore one end and tied the sheet tight. He did the same with his other leg. Taking the next sheet, he drew one end up between his crotch and began to wrap the sheet around the lower part of his body. He tied it around his waist and then tore two long strips from the remaining sheet. He used the strips to encase both his arms, leaving only his fingers out. The rest of the sheet went around his chest, neck, and head until he was completely wrapped, mummylike, with only a slit open for his eyes.

Taking slow, awkward steps, the strange white apparition put one leg into the lake, then the other, and finally sank completely into the water. The sheets grew wet instantly and he felt their water-soaked weight pull on him as he swam with slow, awkward strokes. The sawgrass rose up in front of him and he drew a deep breath as he swam into it. He moved slowly through it, able to touch bottom at places. There was no pull, but he felt the sheets being sliced as if by hundreds of razors. Little ribbons of sliced sheets began to fill the water around him as he continued to push through the vicious plants, and he felt the sheet around his face being sliced open.

He cursed as he felt a sudden sharp pain in one leg. The sheet was in tatters, part of his flesh exposed, and another stab of pain shot through him. The shoreline was close, but the sheets were being sliced to ribbons and his arm felt a sudden tear of pain. He drove forward, aware that the faster he moved, the more the sawgrass would slice into the sheets. But it had suddenly become a desperate race as he realized he needed another layer of sheets around him.

He cried out in pain as two long gashes were sliced into his leg, but the shore was but a few feet away now. He kept his head high as he felt a cut against

143

his shoulders and suddenly he was pulling himself onto the shore, the sawgrass slicing the sheets around his legs in a long, last effort to destroy the invader that had dared challenge its domain. He lay facedown and let his long, deep breaths bring air back into his lungs. When he rose, he saw how completely sliced and torn the sheets were, strips hanging down from all parts of their once-tight wrappings. He had cuts on both legs and arms, one on his shoulder and a few along his left side, he saw as he pulled off the tattered sheets. But none was too deep, and he moved forward toward the rear of the two huts, carrying two long strips of the sheets with him.

He reached the corner of the nearest hut, crept along the side, and dropped to one knee as he peered around the front. One of the Seminoles was but a few feet from him, the next one a few yards away. The Indian was dozing as he stood, Fargo saw, a slight sway to his body. Fargo moved forward on silent steps, one strip of the sheets held outstretched tautly. With one quick motion he wrapped the strip around the man's neck, pulled it tight before the Indian could utter a sound. He held the grip until the Seminole went limp and sagged to the ground. Fargo seized the sentinel's rifle before it hit the ground, a long-barreled old plains musket.

He placed the rifle on the ground, held the second strip of sheet pulled taut as he darted to the next sentry. Once again, the garrote was quick and silent, but this time he had to grab hold of the rifle at once as the man let it fall away quickly. He lowered the figure to the ground, stayed on one knee for a moment to peer at the two sentries before the second hut. They had heard nothing and continued to face forward. He took the long-barrel rifle and hurried forward. As he neared the last two sentries, he saw that both men were standing firmly, back muscles taut. No dozing for these two, he murmured silently. He drew the thin, double-edged throwing knife from the calf holster, held it in the palm of his right hand as he stepped forward.

The Seminole caught a sound and whirled, but just in time to catch the heavy stock of the old rifle as it smashed into the center of his forehead. He dropped instantly, but Fargo, crouched, had already let the rifle fall to the ground and had his fingers around the knife as he saw the last sentry turn at the sound. The Indian started to bring his rifle up. He didn't see the thin blade hurtling through the night at him until it plunged into the base of his neck. He staggered backward, the rifle falling from his hands as he clutched at his neck and then collapsed onto the ground with his legs bent back under him.

Fargo darted forward, retrieved the blade, and wiped it clean on the grass before returning it to the calf holster. He carefully opened the door of the hut and saw the faint flicker of a lone candle. Three young girls lay on the floor, ankles and wrists bound, and their eyes opened as he entered. He put a finger to his lips as they stared up at him, bent down beside the nearest one, and cut her bonds free. He did the same with the others and met their wide-eyed stares of excitement mixed with disbelief.

"Not a sound," he whispered, and they nodded in unison. "Is one of you Una?" A thin girl with straggly brown hair shook her head vigorously. "Annie's with me," he said. "You'll get to see her later. I hope," he added grimly as he rose and motioned for them to follow him. They did so, single-file as he hurried to the next hut and entered. Three more young girls looked up in disbelief at him. "I thought there were seven of you," Fargo said.

"Nora tried to escape along the way," one of the others said.

Fargo swore softly as he freed the three girls and moved from the hut with the six, silent figures following him in a close line. He moved back to the lakeshore, strode along the curve of it to where the line of trees marked the one side of the tract of cleared land. He took the girls into the trees a few yards and halted.

"You stay here. Somebody will come for you. Do exactly as they say, understand?" Fargo ordered, and received six silent nods of understanding. He patted one girl's shoulder reassuringly and hurried away. This time he crossed back through the center of the community to the hut where Carol waited. The moon had reached the far end of the sky, he saw. There were but a few hours left till dawn, maybe less. Carol rose as he entered and took in the half-dried cuts on his body.

"You're hurt," she said. "Let me tend to those wounds."

"No time. They're not bad. Get your things. Time to leave," he said, and Carol followed him out of the hut where he halted and pointed to the far side of the cleared land. "See that line of trees?" he asked, and she nodded. "The girls are in there. You get the horses, go slow around the edge of the land till you reach there, and go inside with the horses. You stay there and keep watching Raynall's place when morning comes. When you see me come down with him, you come out with the girls and the horses, two girls on a horse."

"All right," Carol said, and he watched her hurry away in the darkness before moving in his crouched lope through the center of the tract of land. The moon was beginning to disappear over the treetops of the horizon when he climbed the stone steps. Wavering candlelight came through the lone window of Raynall's hut and he had the six-gun in hand when he pushed the door open. Raynall came into his sight first, seated on a handwoven rug, and Fargo saw the thin, dried trickle of blood that formed a jagged line down his temple. He stepped into the room and saw Annie, her revolver trained on Raynall as she sat across from the man.

Raynall's eyes widened in a moment of surprise as Fargo entered, followed by a half-amused little smile. The man seemed quietly confident, a regal aloofness to him. "You really are part of this. I didn't know whether to believe your hot tempered little friend. I didn't think you were this big a fool," Raynall said.

"Neither did I," Fargo said laconically, and tossed a glance at Annie. "You have any trouble?" he asked.

"Not really, but he fancies himself a real ladies' man," she said.

Raynall interrupted, a weary amusement in his voice. "You can't actually think you'll get away with this," he said. "At a word from me, my people will slaughter you."

"I imagine they will," Fargo said blandly, and saw Raynall's cool amusement disappear into a frown of uncertainty.

Dawn was beginning to push away the night, Fargo saw as he cast a quick glance out the door of the hut.

"I'm ready," Annie said as she saw the tinge of grayness.

"Not yet. I want everybody up and watching," Fargo said, and enjoyed seeing Raynall's frown deepen.

"Maybe you are a lunatic, Fargo," the man said.

"Maybe," Fargo agreed pleasantly.

Raynall stared, his regal aplomb suddenly deserting him. Fargo waited, peered out the door, and watched the community wake, the women first, gathering fruits for breakfast, some brewing tea in stone vessels. The men rose soon after, paused to breakfast before beginning their tasks. Soon most of the Seminoles were up and beginning the day. He drew the Colt from its holster and turned to Raynall. "On your feet," he ordered, his voice suddenly hard steel. The man obeyed and Fargo pushed the gun into his ribs. "Get on the other side of him and put your gun into him," he told Annie, and she obeyed.

"One word from me and you're both dead," Raynall said, not quite successful in summoning up cool calm now as Fargo caught the quaver in his voice.

"That's right. You say that one word and we blow your chest apart from each side," Fargo said. "We'll be killed, but you won't be around to enjoy seeing it. One word, Mister Emperor, one word. It's your call."

Fargo started to the door, moving Raynall along with him, Annie pressing his six-gun into the man's other side.

"What do you want of me?" Raynall asked.

"We're leaving here, Carol, Annie, the stolen girls, and me," Fargo said. "You're going to be our ticket out. You tell the others that you're taking us partway back and you'll return in a day or so. They'll go along with whatever you tell them."

"Yes, they will," Raynall said with a moment of defensive pride in his voice.

"That's the call, mister. We all go alive or we all stay dead. You'll be the first one dead, I promise you that," Fargo said as he went outside with Raynall and started down the stone steps. He and Annie pressed close to Raynall as they walked, the guns into his ribs hidden from view.

"You're risking an awful lot on my going along with you, Fargo," Raynall said. "What makes you so sure I won't sacrifice myself?"

"You're living high on the hog. You're enjoying every damn minute of it. There's no glory in being a dead emperor. Not much fun, either," Fargo said.

"You have it all figured out, haven't you?" Raynall said, a threat coming into his voice.

Fargo swore inwardly. The man was twisted, obsessed with his role. Maybe he would play it out in one grand gesture of defiance. Fargo felt the perspiration coating the palm of his hand folded around the big Colt. He kept his voice nonchalant, almost assured, and realized it took a hell of an effort. "Your call, mister," he said. "Your one word. Your one call."

They were more than halfway down the steps now and he saw the Seminoles gathering, looking up at Raynall. And he saw the movement at the line of trees at the edge of the tract as Carol emerged, the horses and the girls on each one following behind her. She turned along the row of corn and headed to meet him. They reached the bottom, halted, and Raynall ran his tongue over lips that had gone dry.

He pressed the Colt harder into the man's ribs, and Raynall lifted his voice and spoke to the others that had gathered in a half-circle. Fargo couldn't understand any of the Seminole tongue but Raynall was using more than one word, no command in his voice, and he saw the Indians nod their heads. Fargo let a deep breath escape his lips and saw Annie swallow hard. He had won. The gamble was over. He had read the cards right, calculated the measure of James Raynall, and been right. Raynall waved a hand at the Seminoles, a regal gesture, and everyone respectfully stepped back as Fargo and Annie moved on.

Carol and the girls reached them as they walked with Raynall beside them. At Fargo's gesture, they fell in behind. "You won for only one reason, Fargo," Raynall said as they walked. "These people need me. I have too much to give them yet to sacrifice myself."

Fargo's grim smile stayed inside himself. He wasn't about to challenge Raynall's self-justification. Every man needed to give himself reasons for what he did, good or bad, true or false. He'd leave it at that.

They had gone on another dozen yards when the voice called out. "What the hell's going on here?" it asked, and Garson stepped into sight, his two men behind him. Raynall looked at Fargo with a suddenly triumphant smile.

"It seems you forgot about Mac," Raynall said. "An unfortunate oversight."

"No oversight," Fargo said. "I expected he'd show. It doesn't change anything." He halted as the six-guns appeared in the hands of the three men.

"One step more and you're a dead man, Fargo," Garson said.

"That'll make two of us," Fargo said.

"Bullshit. I've a gun on you now. Even you can't draw fast enough to outshoot that," Garson said.

"I don't have to draw. My gun's out," Fargo said. "Fact is it's aimed right at you." Fargo shifted the Colt from Raynall's ribs knowing Annie would keep hers there.

"One of us will get you," Raynall said.

"That's likely," Fargo admitted, but turned his head to look back at the Seminoles who had stopped to watch at Garson's first shout. "But any of you fire one shot and they'll think you're shooting at the king, here. They'll make you look like pincushions in seconds."

Garson's mouth twitched. "Is he right?" he asked Raynall.

"I'm afraid so. It'll all be a matter of instant reaction, too fast for me to stop," Raynall said.

Garson's face twisted as he turned options in his mind. "Then we'll all leave together," he said, and found an oily smile. "It'll be real cozy." He gestured, and one of the men hurried behind the hut and returned leading three horses. Garson and his men mounted and swung in alongside Fargo, Annie, and Raynall. Fargo caught Annie's glance of dismay and kept his face expressionless. Garson's plan was hardly subtle. Once beyond hearing range of the Seminoles, he'd start shooting. Fargo had expected as much, but let himself appear taken aback. There'd be no chance to win until they were away from the Seminoles. Then it would come down to a deadly guessing game.

He saw Raynall smile tauntingly at him. "Do you have the feeling of victory slipping away, Fargo?" the man asked.

"Shut up," Fargo snapped, and fed into Raynall's enjoyment as they moved on. He had gone perhaps another few hundred yards when he called a halt and glanced back at Carol and the girls following in a tense procession. He holstered his Colt and stepped back from Raynall. "No need now to keep a gun in your ribs," he said.

"I'm grateful for small favors," Raynall said, and Annie stepped back and came over to Fargo.

"What're you stopping for?" Garson growled.

"To rest. Those poor girls need it," he said.

Garson snorted derisively but said nothing more, and Fargo felt Annie at his side.

"You know what he plans to do, don't you?" she whispered.

"Same thing I plan to do," Fargo said. "There was no other way to go. We had to get away from Raynall's people or be wiped out. Besides, I have a secret weapon."

"Secret weapon?" Annie frowned.

"You," Fargo said. "Garson doesn't know how good a shot you are. I do. It's going to come down to who decides we've gone far enough. I'm going to see that it's me. I'll take Garson. You take the other two. Don't worry about Raynall. He'll be busy diving for cover. The same for Carol and the girls. Concentrate on Garson's men."

"Got it." She nodded.

"I'll cough. That'll be your signal," Fargo murmured, and then, raising his voice, "Let's move," he called and waved an arm at Carol. He and Annie continued to walk beside Raynall but without their guns in his ribs, and Fargo's eyes were narrowed as he watched Garson. The man turned in his saddle to peer backward. He was trying to decide whether they had gone far enough, and Fargo's eyes stayed on him. Garson turned back and continued forward, but Fargo watched the tension in his jaw. The forest was growing denser with lots of high brush on all sides.

Garson wouldn't wait much longer, Fargo knew, and his eyes stayed on the man. When Garson turned for another look backward, Fargo coughed. He saw Annie spin, drop, and yank at her six-gun. He had the Colt in hand already and saw Garson go for his gun, suddenly aware of what was happening. Fargo fired, the shot whizzing past Raynall to slam into Garson's chest. Raynall dived sideways, flung himself flat on the ground, and rolled, Fargo glimpsed as his second shot followed the first into the exact same place. Garson's chest became a torrent of red as he flew backward from his horse.

On one knee, Fargo saw Garson's two men go down as Annie fired, a quick, accurate volley. One of the men managed a wild shot in return before he clutched at his abdomen and toppled from his horse. Out of the corner of his eye, Fargo had glimpsed Carol dive into the brush with the first shot, and now, still on one knee, he turned to look for her. Raynall had disappeared into the high brush not far from where Garson had gone down, and suddenly Fargo heard Carol's sharp gasp of pain. He whirled again to see the brush move, Raynall's handsome face appear, then, as he rose, Carol's head, the man's arm wrapped around her neck and a revolver at her temple.

"Don't move," Raynall called out.

Fargo stayed riveted in place. "Garson's gun?" he said.

"Yes. I scooped it up as I rolled past him," the man said. "I'm sure he'd approve of my using it."

"Let her go," Fargo said.

"No. She's going back with me. I don't care about the girls. You can take them back," Raynall said.

"Let her go. Otherwise I'll kill you," Fargo said.

"Don't make me do something I don't want to do, Fargo," Raynall said, pressing the gun harder into Carol's temple. "I take her back with me. You take the girls and I never see you again. That's the bargain." Fargo stared at Raynall as he sought a place to shoot. There was none. The man was effectively using Carol as a shield.

"If I say no?" Fargo asked.

"I'll kill her. I don't want to do that. Don't make me," Raynall said.

Fargo half-whispered to Annie, who had come alongside him. "He'll do it. He has nothing to lose now," he said. He raised his voice. "Agreed," he said.

"Throw your guns over here. Both of you," Raynall said, and Fargo tossed the Colt into the brush at his feet. Annie did the same with her gun and Raynall held onto Carol as he bent down and picked up the guns.

"James, don't do this," Carol said. "Forget all this. Come back with me."

"I'm doing what's best. You'll see in time, my dear. You'll be happier than you've ever been," Raynall said. He moved a step backward with Carol. "Go to your horse, Fargo. Throw the rifle down," he ordered. Cursing silently, Fargo went to the Ovaro and put the rifle on the ground. "Now go," Raynall said. "All of you. Don't ever come back."

The girls had all leapt to the ground and Fargo had them mount the three horses Garson and his men had used. He swung onto the pinto and Annie climbed onto the light tan mare. She took Carol's horse along with her as she fell in beside Fargo and he moved forward, the girls following single-file. He glanced back at Raynall and saw the man still holding the gun to Carol's temple as he watched the procession move away. Fargo turned his face forward and led the way through the densely packed trees of the forest. He kept moving slowly for five minutes, until he was well out of sight of Raynall, and then halted and slid from the horse.

"You're going back for her," Annie said.

"You thought I wouldn't?" he grunted.

"No, I knew better," Annie said. "But he's got three guns and a rifle."

"That's right. But he's no marksman and he's running. He's on edge, ready to panic. He thinks he salvaged victory. He'll go wild trying to keep it that way. I've just got to get to him before he gets too close to the Seminoles," Fargo said.

"We'll wait," Annie said.

"No, you go on," Fargo said, and sent the Ovaro into a canter. Anything faster was impossible in the denseness of the forest. Raynall would be moving straight back the way they had come, and Fargo skirted thick cotton gums and tupelos. He made no attempt at stealth. Raynall would hear him in a minute and he wanted it that way. Crashing through the brush, barely avoiding trees, Fargo kept the Ovaro at the canter and Raynall came into sight.

He saw the man turn, fling Carol to the ground, and raise the rifle. Fargo charged at him until he yanked the horse to a halt and dived out of the saddle as Raynall's first shot exploded and hit a tree trunk far off the mark. Fargo landed on both feet in the brush and raced forward, cutting sharply as Raynall fired again. Fargo darted one way, then the other, as he ran in a circle, letting Raynall catch glimpses of him. The man fired again, two more shots, and Fargo swerved, raced directly at him as Raynall threw the rifle down and yanked one of the six-guns from his waist and fired. Fargo flung himself to the ground as three shots went over his head. He rolled noisily and Raynall emptied the rest of the chamber into the brush. But Fargo had come up behind a tree and the shots slammed into nothing but leaves and dirt.

Raynall had the second gun out as he crouched, his eyes wild as they searched the brush. Fargo gathered powerful thigh and calf muscles, leapt from behind the tree, and raced in a zigzag pattern through the trees. "I'll kill you. I'll kill you," Raynall screamed as he emptied the revolver, and Fargo heard the bullets thudding into trees he passed. "Goddamn you, Fargo," Raynall cursed as the hammer clicked against an empty chamber. He flung the gun aside and pulled out the Colt. But suddenly he grew clever and Fargo saw him dart to his left and come up with Carol, yanking her in front of him.

"Come out or I'll kill her. I swear I will, you bastard," Raynall shouted, his handsome face reddened with fear and fury. Fargo stayed silent. The man would follow through on his threat, Fargo knew. He was fighting to survive. That's all that mattered now. He could find other queens. "Come out, damn you or she's dead," Raynall shouted.

Fargo remained absolutely still and watched Raynall's eyes sweep in a wide circle, looking for any sign of movement. The man shouted threats again and Fargo stayed silent, hardly breathing. But his hand slipped down to the calf holster around his leg and he drew out the thin-bladed throwing knife. He waited, listened to Raynall's threats again. He wanted that one moment when the man stepped from behind Carol. It would come, he was certain. Slowly, inching his arm upward, he positioned himself to throw the knife, every muscle in his arm and shoulder tightened.

Raynall began to straighten up, a frown crossing his face. He inclined his head to one side, then the other, straining his ears for any faint sound. "By God, I think I got him," Raynall said, and pulled Carol up with him. "Yes, I got him." Raynall laughed, released his grip on Carol, and she took a half-step away, her face drained of color. "I got him. I got the damn bastard," Raynall said, and began to lower the gun.

Fargo's arm snapped forward not unlike a spring recoiling. The thin blade whistled through the air. Raynall's eyes widened as he suddenly saw it. He tried to twist away, but too late. The blade slammed into the side of his neck all the way to the hilt. Raynall staggered forward, the Colt falling from his hand. Carol screamed and the man clutched at his neck. He managed to get one hand around the hilt of the knife. He pulled, but the strength had already gone from him. His breath a harsh, rasping sound, his fingers fell away from the blade and he fell to his knee, swayed there for a moment, and pitched forward.

Fargo stepped out of the trees and walked forward as Carol ran to him and flung herself against his chest. "Oh, my God, my God," she sobbed.

"There was no other way," Fargo said, and she nodded as she continued to sob. He pulled away from her finally and she stopped trembling as he retrieved the blade and his Colt. He walked to the Ovaro with her, pulled her onto the saddle in front of him. "Time to catch up to the others," he said, and she nodded, unable to find words.

She was silent until he caught up to Annie and the

girls, and he let her slide to the ground. "I never thought it would end this way," she said. "I'd never have come after him."

"Beginnings are one thing. Endings are another. Sometimes they fit well. Most times they don't," Fargo said.

She climbed onto her horse and fell in place behind Annie.

"God, am I glad to see you," Annie said to Fargo. "I was afraid. I really was."

"That's nice," he said. "Now let's ride. It's a long way back to Snakebird."

9

It was indeed a long, slow trip back with the six young girls. But without the tension hanging on everyone, it was pleasant enough, though Fargo had had more than enough of girlish chatter before they reached Snakebird. He avoided the forest people and made a detour around Azard's place, which added another few days to the trip. But he looked forward to the possibilities that waited for him.

It was when Carol was asleep one night that Annie came to him for a moment. "I feel sorry for her. Nothing turned out right," Annie said. "She didn't even get to have you." Fargo half-shrugged and smiled. There were times when silence was best. "When we get back, I'll have the house to myself again. We can really enjoy ourselves," Annie said.

"I'll be keeping that in mind," Fargo said, and she hurried away with a tiny smile of anticipation on her pert face. It was only a few days later, Annie was fixing a loose strap on her cinch, that Carol took him aside.

"She's really a good person under all that bristly surface," Carol said with a glance at Annie. "I'm almost sorry for her." His frown questioned. "She so badly wanted you and she never knew the pleasure of it. She never got to know how great it was." Fargo shrugged again. It was another time for silence. "I'll be heading back to Tennessee. You'll ride with me. Every night can be ours," Carol said.

"I'll be keeping that in mind," he said.

When they reached Snakebird, the first day was taken up with returning the girls to their folks, and he enjoyed a long night's sleep in a real bed at the inn. The next morning, after he'd washed and dressed, he started downstairs and paused when he heard the voices in the lobby, Carol's first.

"Don't make up stories. There's no need for it. I was the one he slept with," she said.

Annie's voice answered. "When, dammit. There was no chance."

"When you were in that coma for three days," Carol said. "I'm sorry but that's the way it was."

"Goddammit, he slept with me first," Annie snapped.

"When? You're lying. There was no time for it," Carol said.

"When the forest people had you. We had plenty of time to wait," Annie said.

"Goddamn," Carol said. "That bastard. He let me think it was only me."

"That's what he let me think," Annie snapped. "That stinking bastard. I believed him, too."

"So did I," Carol said.

Fargo turned. There was a rear way out of the inn and he hurried to it, crept around the side, and dashed to where the Ovaro was tethered at the hitching post in front. He looked up to see Annie and Carol storming out of the inn, one pair of brown eyes blazing, one pair of muted-blue eyes dark with fury. He sent the Ovaro into a gallop as he waved back.

"Fond remembering, ladies," he called as he rode on out of town. It was a wise man who knew when to stay and when to leave, he reminded himself as he headed north, back to the plains country.

LOOKING FORWARD!

**The following is the opening
section from the next novel in the exciting
Trailsman series from Signet:**

THE TRAILSMAN #115
GOLD MINE MADNESS

*Autumn, 1860, the Colorado Territory, when quaking
aspen turned golden and a trek through the mountains
promised mystery and danger at every turn . . .*

The big man astride the magnificent black-and-white
pinto stallion cut his lake-blue eyes to the right and
glanced west once more. The thunderheads he had
watched build since noon had finally moved over the
mountain range into the valley. The still air hung
heavy with moisture; not a leaf stirred, not even the
quaking aspen.

After all he'd been through of late the prospect of
rain represented a welcome relief, although he pre-
ferred not to get drenched to the skin. He had fled
the young widow's house two days ago and left his
poncho behind. The crazy female bedded him on pretense she hadn't slept with a man in over a year, since
her late husband died. At the height of their romp,
just as both were pounding away, straining for the
crescendo, the little bitch asked him to marry her. He
scooped up his clothes and ran without looking back.

The soft sounds of the Ovaro's slow-moving hooves mingled with those made by an unseen shallow stream gurgling over a rocky bottom a short distance on his right. A woodpecker started drilling for a worm somewhere off to his left. The stallion's ears perked and swiveled in the direction of the new sound.

The run-in with Widow Brown was a continuation of a series of pretenses that plagued the big man, pretenses that put him on the trail headed south. He loathed the games people played, especially the widows.

It started in the saloon at Royal Flush, Montana, a small gold-mining town. He caught a man cheating in a game of five-card draw. The nimble-fingered fellow made the mistake of drawing down on him. The big man shot him dead.

There were other "games" the farther south he drifted. Twice in Wyoming Territory he was approached by females on pretense they had been beaten by men. Their stories were so convincing that he took pity on the two women. He sought out and confronted the two woman-beaters, beat the shit out of both. Only to learn the women, in each instance, had lied to him. They were out to get even with the men for rebuking them.

In Grizzly, Colorado, a panic-stricken old man rushed up to him and said he had just been robbed by two men in back of the town's saloon. The old man led him behind the saloon, where the duo stood taking a leak, counting money. The big man didn't ask any questions. He proceeded to beat both to a bloody pulp. He subsequently learned they were counting poker winnings. By that time the old man was long gone with the money.

The widow's game followed two days later.

He glanced west again, wondered if his run of bad luck was over, the promise of an October storm in the high country notwithstanding. The big man sure as hell hoped so.

Powderhorn, his immediate destination, came into view. He saw the little mining hamlet had grown since he last visited it. Back then, only two structures stood: a trading post and next to it a saloon. Both had been shabby then and were even more so now. Silas "Beaver" Trapp built the log and sod-roof trading post, the original structure. When gold was discovered nearby, Miss Comely built the Powderhorn Saloon. Miners named the village after Miss Comely's saloon, which gave them so much pleasure.

Coming closer, he now saw a land and assayer's office had been erected adjacent to the saloon, and next to it a smithy's shop. Across the street, directly in front of the saloon stood a new bank. To the right of the bank was a small general store, also new. Left of the bank, a spacious two-story house was under construction. The yellow-pine framing was up. A shaft of rapidly disappearing sunlight punched through a gap in the mountains and struck the framing, setting it aglow in golden colors.

Hitching the Ovaro to the rail at the saloon, the big man noticed the lack of activity, and thought it odd. Not a horse, buggy, or wagon stood in front of any of the buildings. At this hour he expected to see and hear the hell-raising, boisterous miners. Were it not for lamplight spilling from the saloon into the street, Powderhorn resembled a ghost town. He reckoned the gold mine had played out and the miners had moved on.

As he stepped onto the saloon's porch, a few huge drops of rain pelted, dimpling the soil behind him.

Out of habit, the big man paused at the double doors to look inside before entering. A brawl might be in the making. Or worse, a gunfight. But he saw none of this.

Miss Comely's elderly, shaky bartender, a former gambler who went by the name of Tops, stood behind the bar, cleaning a shot glass. Tops' hands shook so much that he dropped it.

Miss Comely rested the small of her back against the bar's edge across from Tops. She talked in low tones with two older men seated at the table, drinks before them.

The big man recognized one of the men. Gold Pan Jack, a crusty old prospector who had been around for years.

The old fellow occupying the chair across from Gold Pan wore city clothes. The big man reckoned him a businessman, or a wandering drummer.

The only other person in the saloon, a terribly skinny female dressed as a saloon girl, clearly Indian, leaned on the bar down aways from Miss Comely. The Indian appeared bored to tears. She stared blankly at the rack of elk horns mounted on the wall behind the bar.

When he pushed through the swinging doors, all five people jumped, as though a shot had been fired, and turned to face him.

Miss Comely recovered first. Smiling hugely, she said excitedly, "Well, bless my soul if it isn't Skye Fargo. C'mere, big man, and let me hug you."

On pull back, she whispered, "God, but you feel good. Long time no see, Fargo." Strengthening her voice, she said to everyone, "We're going to celebrate the Trailsman's return. Drinks are on the house tonight."

"Make mine bourbon," Fargo told Tops. He watched Tops try to fill a glass. The shaky-handed bartender poured about as much on the bartop as he did filling the glass.

Skinny moseyed up to him. Putting an arm around him, she said, as though a long drought was finally over and might come back within seconds, "Want to have some fun? I buck fast and good."

Miss Comely snapped, "Leave him alone, Lay-Me-Down. Shit, the man just got here. Quit playing with him. You hear me, Lay-Me-Down? I said stop grabbing at Fargo."

Censured soundly by the boss-woman, Lay-Me-Down reluctantly let go of him, turned to Tops, and asked for a mug of beer.

"Ain't no beer," Tops told her. "You know it's all gone. The beer wagon ain't come yet."

Miss Comely snorted, "Hunh! Furthermore the beer wagon ain't coming, either. I told them when they brought the last load not to bring any more." She looked at Fargo. "Powderhorn is drying out. This place is going straight to hell. I don't know if I can hold out much longer, waiting for business to pick back up. Shit, it's bad."

"Did the mine play out?" Fargo questioned.

"Hell, no," Gold Pan barked. "That high-tone bitch is to blame."

Fargo glanced at Miss Comely for her to explain. Hurt and anger filled her voice when she said, "Grace Hatfield. Remember that name, Skye Fargo? Stay away from her, if you know what's good for you."

"What the hell happened?" Fargo quizzed, his brow furrowing.

He watched Miss Comely guzzle from a whiskey bottle. Bristling mad, she explained, "Grace came to

Powderhorn on her personal crusade to give good morals to the misguided, lost sheep, immoral people living on the frontier. Those were the bitch's very words. Misguided, lost sheep, my ass. The hell of it is, those sorry-assed miners went along with Grace." Miss Comely's hazel eyes filled with tears as she looked into his lake-blues and added most bitterly, "Ever' damn one of them got religion. What am I, oh, what am I gonna do, Fargo?"

And that answered that. Fargo had visions of Grace Hatfield being a plump, older woman, a prune-faced, scripture-quoting virgin spinster surrounded by scungy-looking miners bawling their eyes out while listening to her brand of hellfire and brimstone. Fargo did not need or want to hear any of that. He mumbled, "In time, maybe the miners will backslide and fall off the wagon. Most do, you know."

He heard a chorus of relieved sighs escape everyone's lips, then Lay-Me-Down said, "Hope so. I'm getting out of practice."

Fargo looked at her. "Are you Ute? Where did you learn to speak English so well?"

"Yes, I'm Ute," Lay-Me-Down answered. "Beaver taught me."

"By the way, where is Beaver?" Fargo asked.

Gold Pan snorted, "That high-tone female cornered Beaver first cracker out of the barrel. When she started lacing into him, he screamed and hightailed it into the mountains and never came back. I should've gone with him."

"When was that?" Fargo inquired.

"Two months ago," the old gentlemen seated opposite of Gold Pan answered.

Fargo stepped to him. Extending his hand, he smiled and said, "I don't believe we've met."

Rising, the older man gripped Fargo's hand. "My name is Samuel B. Quick. I own the bank across the street." He pumped Fargo's hand slowly, as though it were a great effort.

Fargo felt the weak grip. He said, "I noticed a building going up next to your bank. Looked like a big house. Has construction halted till things return to normal?"

Miss Comely answered venomously, "Yet another mark left by the bitch. I invested every cent I had in building a new saloon. Now all my plans are shot to hell." Tears welled in her eyes when she lamented, "I even paid the passage for six French tarts to come over on a boat. Those tarts are due to arrive here any day now. For the life of me, I do not know where I am going to put them. The crew working on my new saloon caught Grace's religion, too, right along with those sorry-assed miners. They said they weren't about to build such a sinful place, laid down their hammers and saws, and walked off the job. Oh, me, Fargo, what am I gonna do?"

He silently agreed that it was indeed a most sad state of affairs. Still, the high-tone woman had a measure of his respect. Anyone who could corral the otherwise loose morals of miners and construction workers had to be reckoned with.

"Where did she come from, anyhow?" Fargo wondered aloud.

"Pascagoula, Mississippi," Quick answered.

After a long silence, Miss Comely sighed heavily, then said, "Well, enough of this kind of talk. We've bared our rotten, misguided souls to Fargo. He probably won't ever meet up with the woman anyhow." Cocking one eyebrow, as though she might have erred, Miss Comely cut her eyes to Fargo's chiseled face and quickly added, "By the way, where are you headed?"

"Reckoned I'd go south for the winter," Fargo began. "See what's happening in Tucson."

"Tucson?" a voice from behind the double doors asked. "Did I hear Tucson?"

They turned as a shapely, young fiery-red-haired woman pushed her way inside. She carried a parfleche folder under her left arm, a small wooden box in her hand. A smile blossomed on her face as she looked at Fargo through light-green, inquisitive eyes.

"You heard correct, ma'am," Fargo verified. He noticed the others stared nervously at the woman.

"You here on a crusade, or something?" Miss Comely finally asked. "If you are, we don't want to hear about it."

"No, I don't think so," the redhead replied. "This is the only place in town showing light. I've been on the porch waiting for the rain to stop. My name's Maureen. Maureen Bodner." She stepped between Fargo and Miss Comely, set her parfleche and box on the bartop, and ordered a beer from Tops.

"Ain't got none," Tops told her.

Eyeing Maureen suspiciously, Miss Comely said. "What's between the rawhide, girlie?"

"And the box, sweetie?" Lay-Me-Down added, cutely.

"Rum, then," Maureen told Tops. She glanced at Lay-Me-Down, then at Miss Comely.

"The Powderhorn doesn't stock rum," Miss Comely muttered frostily.

The hairs on Fargo's nape perked and started to tingle. The glances the redhead slid to the saloon keeper and Ute might as well have been words that said, You two are trash. And Fargo had also caught

Miss Comely's and Lay-Me-Down's sudden change in attitude the moment Maureen walked in. He wondered if the hairs perking warned him a game had started. Subtle though it was, the three female's body language, coupled with the change in inflection they put in their tone of voice, signaled to him a contest was now in progress. He wondered if their game involved him. With my run of bad luck, Fargo decided, it sure as hell appears that way.

Maureen Bodner continued the game. She smiled when she slid a hand down to Fargo's groin and rubbed, saying dryly, "Stuff. What kind of liquor do you have?"

Now he knew for sure he was indeed involved.

Tops answered, "Whiskey, bourbon, and one bottle of gin."

"Stuff?" Lay-Me-Down echoed, a puzzled expression on her red face.

"What stuff?" Miss Comely asked, obviously rankled. She glanced at the parfleche.

Maureen continued to rub as she said, "Pour me a glassful of bourbon. The parfleche holds sheets of sketch paper, the box my pencils and erasers. I'm an artist, capturing scenes on the frontier, sketching colorful characters living on the edge of civilization."

Lay-Me-Down and Miss Comely shot nervous glances to the rubbing hand. Pain laced Miss Comely's tone when she suggested, "Stop doing that to him. He's tired."

At the same time Fargo said, "No, I'm not," Lay-Me-Down offered, "Dog-tired."

Looking at the big man from over the rim of the glass, Maureen's rubbing ceased. She took a swallow of bourbon, then said to Fargo, "Please bring my folder." She picked up the glass of bourbon and the box, stepped to the two old men's table. Sitting, she tossed Miss Comely a fleeting smile—a put-down if ever Fargo saw one—and said, "I'm going to draw the big man's portrait."

"Mine next?" Gold Pan asked hopefully.

Maureen reached over and turned Gold Pan's head so she could see it in profile. Cocking her head, she squinted one green eye and studied his pose. "Maybe," she mumbled.

"Where do you want me?" Fargo asked.

"Sit across from me so we can share the same light. Would somebody bring a lamp over here?"

Miss Comely and the Ute didn't budge one inch. They didn't have to; the banker and prospector pushed and shoved each other to capture the lamp.

All watched Maureen remove a sheet of drawing paper from the folder and open the box. Then she told Fargo to lean in a tad and fold his arms at the elbows on top of the table. Then she told him to slowly turn his head to the left until she said stop. Having posed him, she started sketching.

Miss Comely's and Lay-me-Down's curiosity got the better of them. They drifted to the table and had a look-see at the sketch and made bitchy comments about the accuracy of Maureen's work. "Not enough chisel to his face," Miss Comely grunted.

"Yeah, and you drawed his nose too small," Lay-Me-Down complained.

"Looks just like the Trailsman to me," Gold Pan corrected.

Maureen asked the banker, "What do you think, Mr. Quick? A tad of highlight on the nose?"

"Maybe. Just a tad, though," Quick agreed.

After about thirty minutes, Maureen declared Fargo's portrait finished. She went to the bar to get a refill of

Tops' bourbon while the others moved around the table to get a better look at the portrait. Miss Comely said it didn't look anything like Fargo. Gold Pan snorted it did, too, look exactly like Fargo. Quick commented she had even drawn the fly that lit on Fargo's shoulder. Fargo said he liked it.

Maureen came back to the table and signed her name on the portrait, printed: POWDERHORN SALOON, MISS COMELY, PROPRIETOR, and dated it SEPT 27, 1860. She glanced up at Fargo and asked, "What did Jack call you? The Trailsman?"

Fargo and Gold Pan nodded.

"What might the Trailsman be?" Maureen inquired.

"A mean bastard." Miss Comely chuckled.

"Then I'll title the portrait, Skye Fargo, The Trailsman."

They watched her print the words just below his portrait.

Miss Comely picked it up, turned the portrait to the lamplight, smiled, and said, "Girlie, I owe you for mentioning the saloon and my name. What can I give you in return for doing such a nice thing?"

Maureen replied faster than a striking diamond-back, "Give me and Fargo a bed to use for a little while."

"You got it," Miss Comely said flatly. "You can use mine. It's already broke in."

"Aw, shit, I missed out again," Lay-Me-Down muttered as she moved to the bar.

"Where is your bed?" Maureen asked. She closed the lid on the box, tucked the portrait inside the par-fleche, then stood.

"Fargo will show you," Miss Comely said.

Apparently I don't have any say in the matter, Fargo thought. He stepped to the double doors.

"Where are you going, Fargo?" Maureen gasped. She hurried to stop him.

Fargo looked at her and nodded toward the street. "Don't get nervous, honey. I'm just checking the weather."

"You scared me," Maureen murmured. She clutched his arm, but did not try to pull him away from the doors.

Unspoken though it was, Fargo reckoned he'd made his point. No verbal point was required. Action spoke louder than words. All it took to stop the bullshit was for him to head for the doors. He didn't know what he would have done if she had called his bluff.

Rain was coming down by bucketsful. Fargo had no intention of getting soaked to the skin. Not when there was a perfectly sound and dry bed in the back room. Still, Maureen and the others had to hear it. Fargo said, "Don't ever take me for granted unless somebody is trying to kill you. Then you can count on my help." He shot the redhead a wink and they left the room.

Miss Comely's room, and the iron bed in it were a pure mess. Clothes were strewn on the floor, hanging out bureau drawers, draped over the headboard, and the sheets on the bed were twisted and rumpled beyond recognition. Only one pillow, Miss Comely's threadbare red velvet rump pillow, lay on the bed. The two regular, goose-down pillows lay where she had thrown them on the floor. Oddly, the straightback chair stood clean as a whistle. Fargo thought the room was perfect for Maureen's and his immediate needs. He closed the door.

The artist couldn't wait for the bed, him or her to undress. Nimble fingers opened his fly as she dropped to her knees. Maureen gasped when she pulled his swelling length out of his fly.

Fargo felt her lips tighten around the mushroomlike ruby-red crown and draw the foreskin down. A hot tongue caressed the blood-swollen bulb momentarily, then licked downward. He heard her gulping and gurgling on his throbbing shaft as she took in more and more of it. He pulled her head back. Her lips were drawn so tight they smacked when he came out.

Maureen cast an excited glance up at him.

He pulled her to her feet, saying, "Undress, then put your shapely ass on that rump pillow." He sat in the straightback to take off his boots.

Maureen stood next to the bureau to quickly shed her clothes. She stood naked before Fargo could pull off the second boot. Gazing at her fiery-hot, bushy patch, he wondered if he was about to enter the gateway to Grace Hatfield's perception of hell. He lifted his gaze to her bosom. Tiny nipples, hardly larger than his own, protruded proudlike from quarter-sized areolae. The breasts, perfectly symmetrical, were milk-white, flecked with freckles, and about the size of small cantaloupes and just as firm.

The redhead knew how to tease, arouse, and excite a man all right, Fargo thought, slipping his Levi's off. He said, "Hop on the bed. Do what I told you."

Maureen was fast to obey. She tucked the pillow under her rump, spread her legs wide, and purred a promise. "Big man, I'm going to give you the wildest ride you ever had."

He believed she would damn sure try. Maureen had all the equipment to do just that. Fargo took one final look at the gates to hell, stood, and moved to the bed.

Maureen greeted him with open arms and legs. He got between the legs and started on the breasts first.

Fargo, too, knew how to tease, arouse, and excite a woman. He nibbled on the nipples, kissed the areolae, love-bit the pillowy breasts before capturing all he could in his mouth.

Maureen trembled, arched her back, and gasped, "Jesus . . . that feels so good. Suck harder . . . bite them . . . Oh, Jesus, Jesus . . . yes, yes, that's it." She began squirming, arching higher and higher. Her left hand went to his head and pressed hard, encouraging him to take in more, while her right hand gripped his hard-on and stroked.

After one final rolling of the tiny, rock-hard nipples between his teeth, Fargo moved into position to find out whether or not the hellcat under him could fulfill her promise.

Her hand moved from his rock-hard, elongated prod to her blood-swollen lower lips and parted them. She moaned, "Take me, Fargo. Oh, yes, take me." She positioned his summit for entry.

Fargo felt the slick opening accept the head. Maureen wanted more than that; she shoved up. Fargo went in about halfway. Moaning joyously, she raised her hips, then her legs, and locked her ankles on his hard buttocks. Fargo thrust all the way in the hot tunnel.

She gasped, through gritted teeth, "Aaagh! Uhmm! So long, so big. I didn't expect . . . Oh, Jesus . . . you're so big."

He felt her heels dig in, her fingernails rake his back. Fargo began gyrating and pumping. Her hips rose even higher and she started bucking, gasping loudly. Soon the semicontrolled thrusts and upward shoves, gyrating and writhing gave way to wild abandon. He thrust pistonlike inside an undersize cylinder.

Both of them were bathed with sweat, their bodies made slapping sounds as they met and pounded.

Fargo felt her first of several contractions seize around his organ.

Lightning flashed on the windowpane. Thunder rumbled into Powderhorn. A fierce wind blew. Hail started pelting the roof.

Four things happened simultaneously: the hellcat screamed, "I'm coming!"; a massive bolt of lightning struck a tree a short distance from the window; Fargo erupted; and a mighty explosion knocked out the windowpane and shook the entire saloon.

Fargo knew at once the bolt of lightning didn't trigger the loud sound. Neither was it caused by thunder.

No, the explosion was man-made.